HOCUS-POCUS UNIVERSE

By
JACK WILLIAMSON

I0541487

ARMCHAIR FICTION
PO Box 4369, Medford, Oregon   97501-0168

*The original text of this novel was first
published by Bell Publications, Inc.*

Armchair Edition, Copyright 2012, by Gregory J. Luce
All Rights Reserved

*For more information about Armchair Books and products, visit our
website at...*

www.armchairfiction.com

Or email us at...

armchairfiction@yahoo.com

THE DAY SCIENCE TOOK A BACK SEAT

Charley Guilborn was a bright young science teacher at a local high school. He knew that two-plus-two equaled four and that the world was guided by basic mathematical and scientific laws. Knowing all this helped Charley and millions of others sleep at night.

Then into the world of facts and figures, of scientists and soldiers, came lonely Eon Hunter. Eon the misfit, whose stubborn refusal to accept the world as it was almost led him down a path to oblivion. Eon the enigmatic, who always returned to involve himself in Guilborn's life. What startling new seed of truth was incubating in the mind of this young genius, or perhaps we should say…wizard?

FOR A COMPLETE SECOND NOVEL, TURN TO PAGE 73

CAST OF CHARACTERS

CHARLEY GUILBORN
This bound-in-earth-science high school teacher leaned that a piece of chalk could do a lot more than write on a blackboard.

EON HUNTER
How could such a total loser and depressed human soul be so instrumental in setting the future course of the Universe?

CAROL WAKEMAN
She was like so many other beautiful women who have men falling all over their feet…she couldn't make up her mind!

DR. ZERLINGER
The future of the United States depended on whether or not he could harness nuclear power in a way never attempted before.

COLONEL FEARING
He was Chief-of-Security for the most critical secret scientific project in America. His job? To trust no one.

DR. MILFORD DRAVEN
The head of Project Light Year. This respected but aging physicist answered only to the President of the United States.

GENERAL BARLOW
He was an old school, tough-as-nails military man, and it was his job to make sure the Russians didn't land the first nuclear punch.

CHAPTER ONE

Carol spoke only to tease me, I'm sure. She was taking my general science course just because she needed a science credit to get her high school diploma; she didn't aspire to become another Madam Curie. Her grades were good enough, but she had more exciting goals. She was seventeen, and just discovering the dark witchcraft of sex.

That was my first year out of college, and I was only five years older. Though I was trying hard to keep the unwritten commandment that teachers shall not have love affairs with their students, she surely knew how deeply she disturbed me.

We were setting up the apparatus for a classroom experiment—a spring gun mounted to shoot a steel ball at a falling weight. I was still too serious about my own small scientific attainments, and I had announced with an unwise solemnity that we were about to demonstrate the universal force of gravitation.

"This magnet drops the weight, as the shot leaves the gun," I had explained, with far too much assurance. "The gun is level. The shot and the weight both move in the same vertical plane. They're both subject to the same gravitational acceleration, which will keep them both in the same horizontal plane. Therefore, no matter what the range is, or how hard we fire the shot, it will always hit the weight."

"Really, Mr. Guilborn?" Bright mischief was shining in Carol's eyes. "I don't believe it!"

"Do you think Newton's laws have been repealed?"

That was a rash question, and Eon Hunter seized it at once. He was a lean, gangling, ungainly youth, a year or two older than Carol. I had been feeling a little sorry for him, because he was so obviously and hopelessly in love with her.

"Why not?" he demanded. "Doesn't everything change?"

His voice was low and serious, almost as if he really meant to challenge Newton, but I saw a quiver of restrained amusement at the corner of Carol's mouth, and heard a stifled titter from the other members of the class.

"We have arranged this experiment to let the laws of nature speak for themselves," I answered hastily. "If the shot does hit the weight, we'll know that the law of gravity is still on the job."

"But it won't," Hunter said.

I looked at him sharply, wondering for the nth time what made him tick. He had been a puzzle to me, and often an exasperation, ever since the first day of school. He was easily my worst student. Yet I knew he wasn't stupid, and I had begun to feel irked at my own failure to interest him in science. He spent the class periods staring vacantly at nothing or filling his notebook with sketches of Carol Wakeman's pretty face. Even his personal appearance annoyed me. He slouched. His hair needed cutting. His shirts were seldom clean. I couldn't understand the fond glow in Carol's eyes when she looked at him—or why he now sat stubbornly shaking his head, as if he really expected the experiment to fail.

"If gravity has quit," I told the class, "you had better hold on to your seats."

Nobody smiled. Hunter straightened at his desk, staring at the suspended weight with a curious defiance in his brooding dark eyes, and I saw that the others had caught his sullen skepticism. Unbelief was vibrant in the room. Even Carol's mischievous eyes had turned grave with doubt.

For a moment I almost lost my temper.

"Hunter is trying to challenge the basic facts of science," I said, too sharply. "But we needn't talk about the question he has raised. Our experiment will pass it on to nature." I pulled back the plunger of the little spring gun. "Just watch the answer."

I released the plunger. The weight dropped. The steel ball flew toward it—and missed.

Somebody tittered.

"Too bad, Mr. Guilborn." Carol was laughing at me. "It looks like Eon is actually repealing your precious laws of nature."

Her laughter made the failure look like a personal victory for Hunter. I was unreasonably upset. I felt my face turning red, and I swung quickly away from the class to replace the weight and pick up the shot.

"I don't think Hunter has really thrown any monkey wrench into the machinery of the universe," I said, when I could trust my voice again. "I imagine the failure was due to another law of science, that I had almost forgotten. It is called Casey's law. It applies to all scientific experiments. It states that everything that can go wrong will go wrong. Perhaps the gun isn't quite level, or not quite in line."

I checked the position of the gun, and tried again. Another miss. A rising titter swept the class. I checked the circuit that dropped the weight. There was nothing wrong that I could discover, but the shot kept missing. I was trembling with a futile exasperation, before the bell rang.

Most of the students seemed merely amused at my misfortune, as they filed out of the room, but Hunter's gaunt face wore an awed elation. He paused silently to look at the apparatus, and then marched solemnly on as if lifted up with the secret awareness of some irresistible power.

Carol stopped at my desk.

"I'm sorry, Mr. Guilborn. I didn't intend to embarrass you."

She smiled, and I forgave her everything.

"And, please don't stay mad at Eon."

"I'm trying not to be angry," I told her. "But I certainly don't understand him."

"Nobody does." Her voice softened tenderly. "But I like him anyhow."

When she was gone, I hooked up the weight and the gun one more time in the very same way and repeated the experiment. The prompt ping of the shot against the falling weight assured me that Newton's laws were once more in force. I resolved to forget my chagrin and try to understand Eon Hunter.

That was hard to do, but he caused me no more trouble in class. Next day he sat sprawled as idly as usual in his seat, staring out of the window at the gaudy colors of fall on the hills around Picton, seeming to hear nothing I said. It seemed wiser not to disturb him.

A few weeks later, I called at his home. He had just failed the midterm examinations in nearly all his subjects. I thought that his lack of attention and effort might be due to some personal difficulty that I could help him solve.

Secretly, too, I must have been still hoping to discover how he had managed to defy the law of gravity.

My landlady told me where he lived, and supplied a gossipy history of his parents.

"They've come down in the world so far it nearly kills 'em," she said. "Lucinda Hunter's from somewhere in the South. Never had a penny, as far as I know, but she can't get over all the slaves and plantations her people owned a hundred years ago, before the Civil War. She thinks she's a little too good to mix with us common folks, here in Picton."

"And what about Eon's father?"

"A good enough match for her, I guess. Old Caleb Hunter's grandpa was one of the first pioneers to stake out his claim in the Picton Valley. When I first remember Caleb, his pa was still well to do, with the biggest store in town and a fine house on Broad Street. He's nothing but a bookkeeper now, in the store his daddy used to own."

Broad Street was blighted now, with the fine old homes sagging into decay. A dead tree spread its whitened limbs over a yard of dead weeds beside the old Hunter house. The rotten shutters had fallen apart, and the front porch groaned alarmingly under my feet.

Eon's father came to the door in a soiled kitchen apron, with a dishrag in his hand. He was a tired little man, with a pinched red face and a feeble smile of false optimism. I caught a whiff of whisky on his breath. He gave me a damp, limp hand, and took me back into the gloomy old living room.

"Ma!" he called, with a hollow heartiness. "Look who's here! The science teacher Eon was telling us about."

I didn't ask what Eon had told.

Lucinda Hunter sat in a wheel chair, reading a tattered magazine. Her thin body was hunched with arthritis. Her hands were painfully swollen and twisted. Only her face seemed unmarked with suffering. She looked up at me with a vague fleeting smile, like that of a happy child unwilling to be drawn from some exciting private game.

I asked about Eon.

"He said he was going for a walk," she told me. "The trees are so pretty, this time of year. If I could only get out—"

She shrugged stiffly, with a faint smile of sweet resignation.

"The boy's always hiking off, all by himself," Caleb Hunter added. "Sometimes out till midnight. Just walking and thinking, he says. I don't know where he goes, or what he finds to think about."

That looked like the opening I wanted.

"I'm worried about him," I said. "He's not attentive in class. I'm afraid he isn't trying—"

"Why should he try?" Hunter's voice sharpened. "What can he look forward to, in times like these?"

"These times aren't really so bad for young people who accept them realistically," I protested. "I don't think many things are actually impossible to a young man like Eon, if he's only willing to make the necessary effort. You are doing him a serious wrong, if you deny him hope."

"Hope?" The worn little bookkeeper gestured with the greasy dishrag, as if erasing hope. "He'll be drafted next year. If he gets home all in one piece, he'll have to drudge the rest of his life away at some dull two-bit job. He hasn't got a chance."

I tried to tell him that Eon could surely find or create some opportunity to do whatever he wanted, but his black pessimism made my words sound like empty platitudes. I turned to Lucinda Hunter.

"I'm only trying to help your son find himself," I told her. "Doesn't he have some gift? Some special interest that we can help him find and cultivate?"

"Eon has many talents." Her smooth face reddened, as if I had stung her pride. "More than you can imagine." She moved her head stiffly to look at her husband. "Show Mr. Guilborn Eon's paintings."

Caleb Hunter took me upstairs to Eon's room. Books were stacked on the unmade bed. They were piled on the rickety desk, and scattered among odds and ends of soiled clothing across the dusty floor. A thin reek of turpentine and linseed oil met us at the door, and I saw a covered easel placed where it would catch the north light from the window.

I paused to glance at Eon's books. Tattered old volumes of Sir Walter Scott, which must have come down from his mother's Southern family. Victor Hugo and Edgar Allan Poe. Shakespeare, Browning, Keats. Classics. But nothing that could have taught him how to suspend the laws of motion.

"Always got his nose buried in some moldy old book." His father sniffed. "He can't afford the new ones, but mostly he's happy enough with these. Till he gets his moody spells."

He was gathering up books and muddy shoes and tubes of drying paint, so that we could reach the easel. I asked if Eon had taken art lessons.

"Only from his mother. She used to paint, before her hands got so bad. Did illustrations for children's books. She taught him a lot, before he got so discouraged."

He reached for the cover, and suddenly paused.

"But he never showed her this one. He's—well, funny about it. He always turned it to the wall, when I came in and found him working on it. So don't let on you ever saw it."

He uncovered the painting.

"Oh!" I had to catch my breath, because it was so completely unexpected. A lovely girl sat on a rock in the foreground of a fantastic prehistoric landscape, feeding flowers to a hideous reptile.

"Well?" Hunter's small bloodshot eyes were almost apprehensively intent. "What about it?"

Ordinarily, I preferred the abstract paintings that seemed to reflect the mathematical abstractions of science and the clean geometry of modern machines. Eon's fantasy seemed illogical and unscientific. The great reptiles were all extinct, I knew, many million years before the human race evolved. I thought the smiling girl should logically have been afraid of that many-fanged beast. I felt that I shouldn't like the picture at all.

Yet it caught hold of me, with its reckless mood of pure romance. My common sense struggled against the spell of fantastic gayety it cast over me, and surrendered to something stronger than fact or logic. Suddenly I wanted to deny all the uncomfortable realities I knew, and escape the drab world around me to join that happy girl in her enchanted universe.

"It's beautiful!" I told Hunter. "I don't pretend to know what it means. And of course I'm no critic. But I think it's wonderfully done. Amazing, to be the work of a high school boy. Eon certainly ought to go ahead with his painting."

Caleb Hunter seemed somehow displeased at my enthusiasm.

"Go ahead?" His nasal voice lifted sharply. "You don't know how crazy he is, about this picture. He says it came to him one night in a dream. He worked on it for months, getting it just the way he wanted it. Now he says he's got nothing else to paint."

He moved impatiently to replace the cover over the painting, but I caught his arm to stop him. I wanted to look at the girl again. She was nude, except for a wreath of the same strange flowers she was feeding to the snarling monster. Her face and figure were idealized, but I had recognized her.

"Did Carol—" Something choked me. "Did Carol Wakeman pose for this?"

"I wouldn't think so!" Caleb Hunter seemed somewhat shocked. "A nice girl like her. Not here in a nice quiet little town like Picton." He backed away from the picture, squinting at it. "But since you say so, it does look like her. If she was a few years older, and—well, undressed like that."

"No matter," I muttered. "It's really no business of mine."

Yet I felt numb and cold with loss, as if Eon had somehow taken Carol out of my reach forever, beyond logic and reality, to that luminous dreamworld of his painting.

"That's her, all right." Hunter squinted again, and scowled disapprovingly. "Maybe she did pose for him. They've been in love for years. Such a pity, for Eon."

"Why?" I wrenched my attention from the painting. "Why shouldn't they be in love?"

"What good can ever come of it?" Hunter shrugged hopelessly. "You know how it is, with kids their age. Eon hasn't got a dime. We couldn't spare a cent to help 'em get a start. Anyhow, he'll soon be drafted. In four or five years, maybe, if he happens to get back alive—" He interrupted himself, with a tired little gesture of bitter futility. "But he won't ask her to wait. He says it wouldn't be fair to her."

"Maybe that's the difficulty I was looking for." I nodded. "If Eon feels that way—"

"Shhh!" Hunter lifted his hand, and I heard the old stairs creaking. "That's Eon!"

He moved with a guilty haste to cover the painting, but he was too late. Eon burst into the room, snatched the cover, and flung it over the easel.

"Don't—" The boy was white and gasping with an unaccountable fury. "Don't show that to anybody!"

Caleb Hunter cringed away.

"Now, son," he protested weakly. "Don't get mad. Mr. Guilborn came just to try and help you—"

"I don't want help," Eon snapped. "Just leave me be!"

"I didn't intend to intrude," I said clumsily. "But I can see that you must be struggling with some personal problem. I was hoping—"

"You stick to your precious science," he broke in hoarsely. "I'll take care of my own affairs."

CHAPTER TWO

His father and I retreated. He slammed the door behind us, but I had seen the tears welling into his tortured eyes. The sound of his sobbing followed us down the stairs. His father let me out, with a whispered apology.

That strange outburst left me deeper than ever in the dark about Eon and his secret difficulties. He came to my office before class next day, and told me stiffly that he was sorry. That was all. He didn't offer to explain anything, and his sullen reserve made it clear that he would tolerate neither questions nor sympathy.

His moody spells were darker and more frequent as the term went on. He sat brooding through my lectures, as if his mind were a million miles away—or sixty million years, perhaps, in that prehistoric world where he had painted Carol.

He kept failing. I began to suspect that he was near the breaking point in his own lonely struggle.

I wanted to help him—partly, perhaps, to atone for the jealousy that I could never quite escape—but I didn't know how.

When the spring term began, he didn't come back to school. Carol told me that he had been rejected for the draft. She said he was looking for a job, and soon I saw him driving a delivery truck for the department store where his father worked.

Carol seemed as deeply bewildered and distressed about him as his parents had been when I talked to her. She was having occasional dates with him, she told me, but he must have been a pretty grim companion.

In spite of all Mr. Baxter's hints that teachers and students must not allow themselves to become too intimate, I was seeing a good deal of Carol. Her home was near my boarding house, and I began timing myself to walk with her or pick her up in my old car on the way to school and back. Sometimes we stopped for a Coke. For her part, she began coming into my office to ask about science problems that I knew she already understood. She no longer questioned the law of gravity, even to tease me.

One spring day when we were alone in my office, I started impulsively to tell her how much I was coming to love her. She seemed pleased, but disturbed. Her face colored deeply, and she caught quickly at my arm to stop me. I felt her fingers trembling.

"Wait, Charles!" Her level eyes looked into mine, turning slowly bright with tears. "I like you, too. An awful lot. But I've got to tell you—" She stopped to catch her breath. "I'm engaged to Eon."

"Oh!" I stammered lamely that I wished them happiness. "And when is the wedding?"

"I don't know, Charles." Her voice was choked with trouble. "We had planned it for right after graduation. Eon got this job, and my folks promised to help us. But then something happened."

She stood silent for a moment, looking pale and miserable.

"Something horrible!" she went on with a rush. "Eon's mother somehow got out of her wheel chair and up into his room. She found a painting of his that I had posed for. It upset her terribly. She tore the canvas to shreds. And then she must have had some kind of stroke. She was lying moaning on the floor when Eon came in. She seems terribly jealous of me now, and Eon says we'll just have to wait till she gets over it."

"You're crazy, if you wait for Eon." I had forgotten Mr. Baxter's commandment. "I do love you, Carol. I want you to be happy. But I don't think you could be with him. He's too much like his parents. They aren't—well, normal. They can't take the world as it is. They're all living back in the past. Or somewhere else—"

I broke off, wondering suddenly about that prehistoric landscape where Eon had painted Carol. If he refused so stubbornly to accept the hard facts of science, where had he got his dinosaurs?

"Eon is different from other people," Carol agreed quietly. "Because he's a genius. A real genius! He'll do something tremendous, if he ever finds himself—though maybe not in painting or literature. But he hasn't found himself yet. He's terribly unhappy. He needs me, Charley. He says he needs me desperately. I'm sure I love him—though he sometimes seems so strange!"

Until then, I hadn't realized how deeply I had let my emotions get involved with Carol and her peculiar genius. I didn't sleep that night. By morning, I had decided to leave Picton and look for other interests.

I found them.

When school was out, I said goodbye to Carol as casually as I could, and went back to the university to finish my graduate work. One of my professors was the great Dr. Zerlinger. He introduced me to the mystery and drama of research. He let me help with some of his own exciting work in atomic fusion, and the summer after I received my own doctorate, he took me with him to the hush-hush conference where Project *Light Year* was launched.

The secret invitations had come from the White House, and our host was Dr. Milford Draven, the distinguished physicist who was then the President's special assistant in matters involving science. We met at a resort hotel in Florida, behind a screen of plainclothes guards. General "Buster" Barlow and his staff; a team of State Department experts; a few picked industrial executives; two dozen of the top American scientists.

Nobody seemed to know why we were there, and the rumors seemed fantastic then. General Barlow was a restless little bundle of steel and dynamite. He rechecked our identifications, pinned badges on us, and indoctrinated us in the military security regulations with a cold-eyed efficiency that quenched all nonsense. When we were all assembled in the hotel ballroom, Dr. Draven rose to speak.

"Perhaps you have been amused at this cloak-and-dagger atmosphere."

He was a frail old man leaning on a cane, and it was hard where I was seated to catch his halting words. "You won't be amused, when you see why it's necessary. The facts are simple—and frightening. Our country is in danger. Your job is to save it."

He paused to mop at his haggard face—the room was not air conditioned, and the summer heat was oppressive.

"The President regrets that he is unable to be here himself," Draven went on. "His message to you is that he is placing the safety of the nation in your hands. Now we shall begin our consideration of this very grave crisis, with reports from the departments of State and Defense."

A whole panel of experts briefed us. An intelligence officer told us that a long series of trans-oceanic rockets, carrying atomic warheads, had been tested in Siberia—upon inhabited towns. The puppets of the Kremlin were pushing forward everywhere. The cold war was thawing fast.

With a hot war in prospect, General Barlow informed us our own weapons were sadly inadequate. We had nothing fast enough to intercept those atomic rockets. A strong offense was the only possible defense, but even there we were dangerously unguarded.

"We do have adequate stockpiles of nuclear weapons in all types," the general said. "Unfortunately, as things stand now, we can't deliver them. Our aircraft can be intercepted. Even our newest rocket missiles lack the necessary range. As things stand today, we are helpless in the face of the enemy."

Buster Barlow and his officers sat down. Dr. Draven limped back to the platform and cleared his ancient throat.

"That's our problem, gentlemen," his old voice quavered. "As scientists, you must already see what answer we must find. We must have atomic power to deliver our own atomic missiles and to intercept the enemy's—"

"We have atomic power," somebody put in.

Draven shook his cadaverous head.

"Unfortunately, our crude atomic heat engines, designed to run aircraft and surface craft and submarines, have all turned out to be short steps in the wrong direction. They all waste atomic energy to heat air jets or to generate steam. It must be applied directly."

He gestured feebly to silence a mutter of protest.

"You have been called together as a scientific team, working directly under the President in this grave national crisis, to design and develop a true nucleonic power plant."

"Impossible!"

Half a dozen atomic scientists and rocket engineers were on their feet, clamoring to say why true atomic rockets could never be built. The best possible rocket motors burned out fast enough in the feeble heat of ordinary chemical fuels. No conceivable motor could contain and control nuclear fuels, reacting at a hundred million degrees.

"You might as well ask us to build a ship out of water or a gun out of gunpowder." Dr. Zerlinger summed up the arguments, wryly. "The known principles of science state that it can't be done."

"It must be done," General Barlow answered with a bleak authority, as if he were ordering us to storm some enemy hill. "If you can't do it with any known principles of science, then you'll have to invent some new ones."

I suppose, in a way of speaking, that is precisely what we did. The conference had dragged on for days. Every hopeful suggestion had been promptly demolished, until one dreary morning, after another sleepless night, when I was sitting with Dr. Zerlinger in the guarded dining room. We were both groggy with fatigue and nicotine, and I was saying that we ought to give it up and turn in.

"Not yet, Charley. Zerlinger pushed the empty coffee cups and full ashtrays aside impatiently, as if he meant to design a space ship on the stained tablecloth. "You've got a brain. That's why I brought you down here. Use it. Forget all our false starts. Look back at the basic problem. How can we make reacting nuclei push a vehicle?"

"Maybe we can do it with magnets."

I claim no credit for that automatic response. I wasn't really thinking, but only wondering vaguely how to get away from Zerlinger, and whether a shower would be worth the effort before I went to bed. But an unexpected interest flickered in his tired eyes.

"How?"

I turned the idea over to see what had caught his attention.

"Take the reaction of hydrogen and lithium." I spoke almost at random. "The two nuclei fuse to make two high-speed alpha particles. Magnetic fields deflect alpha particles. With the right arrangement of strong enough magnets, we could channel them into an atomic jet that would propel a ship."

"Good enough." He leaned restlessly across the table. "Other people have thought of that. But how are you going to make the hydrogen and lithium react in the first place—without a uranium bomb to touch them off?"

"We might do it with the same magnetic field." I was still too dull with weariness to think of all the inevitable objections to what I was proposing. "We'll ionize the fuel atoms. Make 'em collide at reaction velocities."

"Won't work." Zerlinger scowled across the cluttered table. "The cross sections are too small."

"Then we'll magnify the cross sections," I said. "With a stronger magnetic field."

"How is that possible?" His glazed eyes blinked uncertainly. "No relationship has been established between nuclear cross section and magnetic field intensity."

"Because nobody has tried a strong enough field." I was suddenly wide-awake, aroused by a flood of faith in my own idea. "That means the effect must be close to zero, with ordinary fields—but it ought to vary with the cube of the field intensity. Here, I can write the equations for that."

I jotted the symbols on a paper napkin. Zerlinger peered at them owlishly. A spark of conviction lit and brightened in his hollowed eyes.

"You've got it, Charley!" He stood up drunkenly, folding the napkin with quivering fingers. "I'll take this to Draven. If you're so worn out, you can go on to bed."

I went to bed. Before I woke that steamy afternoon, Zerlinger had converted the skeptics. Nuclear physicists had begun to recall laboratory effects that tended to prove the Guilborn equations. The conference was already planning the details of Project *Light Year.*

Within a few weeks we were in New Mexico, staking out the sites for our shops and testing grounds on a high, bare table-mountain. Barbed wire went up to protect our secrets. Construction men and engineers swarmed into the astonished little town of Valdes, under the mesa.

Carol's letter came to me there, addressed in care of General Engineering, the dummy corporation we had set up to conceal the project. I thought I had forgotten her, yet my breath caught when I recognized her delicate script. She wrote:

Dear Charley:

I have been pressing Mrs. Standefer, your old landlady here, for all bits of news she gets about you. She gave me your new address, and I hope you won't be too much surprised to hear from me.

You may be interested to know that Eon Hunter and I never got married, after all. Since his father's unexpected death last year— from a heart attack, as Mrs. Standefer may have written you—Eon is left to take care of his mother. With her feeling the way she does toward me, and her health so bad too, Eon decided that our marriage couldn't possibly work out. We've broken off the engagement—this time, for keeps!

Now I want to get away from Picton. I'm just finishing a business course, and I'm wondering if you could recommend me for a secretarial position—anywhere but here! I can take dictation and type 80 words a minute.

Yours hopefully, Carol

PS:
I often think of you, and I felt very happy when Mrs. Standefer told me about your new position with General Engineering. It sounds important!

CHAPTER THREE

Perhaps I should have recalled how unaccountably she and Eon had sabotaged that experiment in my general science class, because Project *Light Year* was still nothing more than a billion-dollar experiment in a newer field of physics—and already giving us trouble enough.

But I didn't think of that.

I couldn't help wanting to see Carol again, and it was easy enough to get her a job on the project. My heart began to thump when I saw her getting off the plane—the mischievous schoolgirl had bloomed into something far more exciting. There was no Mr. Baxter to lift an eyebrow when he found us together on the dusty streets of Valdes. I saw her as often as I could escape my job, even though she warned me candidly that she still had a soft spot for Eon.

"I'm sorry, Charley." We had parked on the rim of the mesa, outside the barbed wire, and she sat for a moment staring wistfully out across the brown desert at the ragged blue mountains eighty miles away. "I know Eon's hopeless. A born misfit. But he's hard to forget."

"Is he worth remembering?"

"He is." Tears filled her eyes. "He really is!"

When we got back to her apartment, she had me come in to see her scrapbook of Eon's poems. I leafed through them while she was in the kitchenette mixing us a drink. Most of them were manuscript copies. A few had been clipped from minor magazines. I didn't bother to read any of them—I don't care for most verse, and I was prepared to dislike these efforts in particular. I saw that they were signed EON—all in capitals, an arty-seeming touch that annoyed me. I closed the book with relief when Carol brought the drink.

"Do read them," she begged. "They'll help you understand how I feel about him. He doesn't fit into the world, but he never let it crush him—that's the spirit you have to admire. In his own way, he has been creating his own new worlds. Worlds where beauty and splendor and courage really belong."

Reluctantly I started reading something that turned out to be a love lyric addressed to Carol herself. It had a fire and feeling that stabbed me with a savage jealousy. I said as calmly as I could that it was very pretty, and gave the book to Carol. She opened it again, to read a few other passages aloud. Though I was not a very willing listener, her tender voice gave the words an unearthly beauty that somehow recalled Eon's strange painting of her and that prehistoric reptile.

"Isn't he magnificent?" she whispered eagerly. "Tragic, of course. But still magnificent! He has taken the whole world for his enemy, but he never surrenders. Even when he feels trapped and imprisoned, he's always in rebellion."

"I guess he does have some ability," I muttered grudgingly. "But, it's pretty hard to make a living out of writing, I'm told. Most of these poems weren't even published."

"That's the pity of it." She closed the book, with a sigh. "Eon says the modern world isn't geared for poetry. Only for mass production and mass destruction. He says poets and artists will soon be extinct, like the old dinosaurs. Unless things change."

I wasn't expecting any change, but Eon himself was far from extinct. I was fighting him for Carol, with all the time I could take from the project, but even in Picton he remained a formidable rival. When he came to Valdes, I thought that I had lost her again.

The project was consuming all my exertions. We were lagging behind schedule. Our specifications called for new magnetic alloys and new superconductors that always seemed impossible until the bad news in our secret intelligence reports forced us to invent them.

That autumn Sunday, however, Dr. Zerlinger had let me off. Carol and I drove to the mountains and ate our picnic lunch on a granite crag high above the slopes of golden aspens. For a few light-hearted hours, I forgot the danger of war and the shadow of Eon. But he was waiting for Carol when we got back, sitting asleep in the little patio outside her apartment.

His gaunt face was dark with an untidy stubble of beard, and his grimy clothing looked as if he had ridden the freight trains all the way from Picton. Probably he had. He awoke when be heard us and stood up stiffly, grinning at Carol.

"Eon!" She ran to meet him with a breathless joy that hurt me like a knife. "Darling! I'd no idea—Is anything wrong?"

"Mother died two weeks ago," he told her. "I suppose I was pretty badly broken up at first. I had to get away from Picton." He looked ruefully down at himself. "I know I shouldn't have come out here in this shape. But I'm— well, broke. There was nowhere else."

Though I wasn't quite delighted to see him, I tried to be civil. I took him to my room for a drink and a bath, and outfitted him with clean underwear and an old suit of mine, while Carol cooked supper for him.

She called me later that night and asked me to get him a job. That took some doing. Our table of organization at the project didn't call for poets—or even for common laborers, now that the construction work was done. Finally I got him on as a janitor in the spaceframe shop.

He had not been cleared for the guarded and restricted areas where we were at work on the experimental nucleonic motor, but the day he saw the half-finished hull of the *Light Year* lying in the cradle, he came up to me as I left the gate.

"Wait, Guilborn!" He was flushed and out of breath with an excitement that seemed somehow defiant. "I want to talk to you. Isn't this a spaceship you're building?"

"You've been told about security," I warned him rather curtly. "If you start asking too many questions or talking too much about anything you may happen to see—you'll soon find yourself in serious trouble."

"I'm not a spy!" His lean face darkened. "But any fool could see you're working on an interplanetary ship." He caught anxiously at my arm. "What I want is a place aboard."

That startled me. "Why?"

"Because I despise this world we're trapped in." His low voice trembled with a stifled savagery. "This ugly world! It has always robbed me of everything I wanted. It's fighting to crush me now. I'd risk anything to get away from it—even just to the moon or Mars!"

"I doubt that they're looking for space jockeys, right now," I told him noncommittally. "Anyhow, I'm afraid your notions are a little too poetic. The first spacemen will have to be scientists, and they won't be running away from this world. Their survival will depend on how much of it they manage to take with them."

Then, unwisely, I tried to give him a piece of advice. "I guess things have been hard for you. But don't forget that lots of people are moderately happy, even in this world you hate. I believe you're still young enough to adjust yourself."

He walked on beside me toward the parking lot without speaking, and I thought that he was listening.

"By the way, we have a man here on the staff I'd like for you to see." I was trying to sound casual. "Even in this imperfect world, you'll find that science can help solve some of the problems it creates. Dr. Fineman is a pretty good psychiatrist. If you'll let me see about an appointment—"

"Certainly not," he broke in harshly. "I'm not interested in cutting and trimming myself to fit whatever you and Dr. Fineman think I ought to be. Thanks, all the same. But if anything has to be adjusted, I prefer to adjust the world and not myself."

That sounded like nonsense, and I told him so.

"You're the crazy one!" he flared at me. "Living in your own crazy dreamland! Just wait, and I'll show you!"

He stalked angrily away to catch his bus.

I had the evening off, but when I phoned Carol she told me that Eon was taking her out to dinner. I went rather morosely back to the shop and helped Dr. Zerlinger run the preliminary tests on a new paramagnetic alloy. Carol was calling when I got back to my room at midnight. She was sobbing into the phone, and she wanted to know if I had quarreled with Eon.

"He stood me up!" she gasped. "Never even called. You know him, Charley—how strange and moody he is. I'm so frightened about him! Where could he be?"

Drunk somewhere, I thought. But I didn't say so. I went with Carol to the house where we had found him a room. He wasn't there, and Mrs. Montoya knew nothing about him. We checked the three bars in Valdes, but he had not been seen.

He didn't report for work next morning. The project security officers failed to find him anywhere. They questioned Carol about him, and grilled me as if they almost suspected that I had planted him to steal information for the Kremlin. Fortunately, he had not been inside the secret shops, and I felt certain that no harm had been done.

Only a few weeks later, however, General Barlow called us out of the shops to an emergency meeting at the headquarters building. When we were packed into a guarded conference room, he stalked to the speaker's stand.

"Some blabber-mouthed fool has leaked!" His drill-field voice was brittle with wrath. "Or else some damned spy has sold us out. Listen to this!"

He jerked his head at Colonel Fearing, the quiet little security chief, who was standing by with a tape recorder. There was a wail of funeral music, and then a doom-laden voice began to proclaim that the American capitalistic-reactionary atomic murderers were preparing their crowning atrocity against the defenseless peoples of the world.

"The latest propaganda blast across the Iron Curtain," the general rasped. "Our monitors picked up this English-language version last night."

"—red-handed lackey scientists paid by the Wall Street gangsters have set up this new murder-laboratory in the American desert, near the village of Valdes," the machine ran on. "They are building an atomic fusion reactor, of a new and criminally dangerous type. With it, they are preparing to murder every living thing on Earth.

"Even themselves!

"It is known that this new atomic murder device has been designed to start a hydro-lithium nuclear fusion reaction in a solution of lithium salts. Apparently these pig-headed American atomic murderers are determined to ignore one terrible fact which was pointed out today by a peace loving Soviet atomic scientist. That deadly fact is this—all the oceans of the Earth are actually dilute solutions of lithium salts.

"These American atomic murderers are preparing to detonate the whole Earth, unless their criminal experiments are halted by prompt action from the peace-loving peoples of the democratic Soviet nations."

The angry general raised his hand, and Colonel Fearing shut off the machine.

"Lies!" Barlow barked. "The same old stinking lies. Actually, as most of you know, the lithium content of sea water is excessively small, and I have been assured a hundred times by competent authorities that the hydro-lithium reaction cannot possibly maintain itself outside the fusion field. In fact, we're still far from sure that we can maintain it anywhere, even inside the reactor."

He caught his breath, glaring at us.

"Yet these particular lies are extremely dangerous to the project, and to our whole defense program, because they have been wrapped so cleverly around a core of fact—the key secret that we have allowed some fool or traitor to betray. They are doubly dangerous, because we can't deny them."

"Why not?" Zerlinger inquired.

"Because we've no idea how much secret information has been compromised." Barlow glowered at him. "We must assume, however, that if the commissars knew how to build a fusion reactor of their own, they'd keep quiet and build it. Since they didn't, they're pretty obviously fishing for more information.

"You see we can't say anything at all, without giving them more. Any departure from our established policy of simply ignoring such charges would at least confirm the existence of Project *Light Year*. Our lips are sealed.

"But we must stop that leak!"

As the spy-hunt began, I recalled Eon Hunter's defiant declaration that he was going to adjust the world instead of himself. Now his words had an ominous ring. It seemed conceivable to me that his twisted bitterness had made him a dupe of the Communists, and I took my suspicions to the security officers.

They interrogated me all over again, dredging up everything I could recall about Eon's habits and associates. I knew that they would go from me to Carol, and that night I stopped at her apartment to find out how she had stood the ordeal. She came to the door with tearstains on her face, and she whitened with anger when she saw me.

"You jealous fool!" Her voice was choked and bitter. "What have you done now?"

"Nothing so bad." I shrugged. "If Eon's innocent, he can clear himself. But if he is, I'd like to know why he ran away."

"You've never understood him," she whispered savagely. "You're not fit to!" Her voice lifted hysterically.

"He's no spy! And I'll always hate you for trying to tattle on him."

"Please, Carol." I stepped toward her in the doorway. "You're all keyed up. Let's go out somewhere for a drink—"

She stopped me with a stinging slap.

"Get out!" she gasped. "I never want to see you again!"

The door slammed in my face.

But she called me late one night, not two weeks later. Her voice was hoarse from crying. She hadn't heard from Eon, and she was making up her mind to get over him again.

"I'm terribly sorry that I slapped you, Charley," she whispered. "Because I guess that you were right. I know Eon has always hated the world he was born into. I'm afraid he wouldn't stop at anything to smash what he hates."

Her slap wasn't hard to forgive. She let me come by for her. We had two drinks in a bar, and drove out on the mesa. We didn't stay long. She was trying a little too hard to be gay, and she broke into tears when I kissed her.

"I can't help it, darling," she sobbed. "All this isn't very fair to you. But I just can't get over Eon."

Colonel Fearing told me a few days later that the federal agents had found Eon, without too much difficulty. It turned out that he had simply walked away from Valdes in an all-consuming fit of depression, and hitchhiked to New York City. He was living there under his own name, and he soon convinced the investigators that he had never betrayed or even learned any facts about the hydro-lithium reactor.

Far from attempting to destroy the profit system, so he told the federal men, he had decided to make the best of it.

He had given up his forlorn dabblings in poetry and art, and found a job with an advertising agency. Surprisingly, his new employers valued him highly. When they came to his defense, the investigation was dropped.

CHAPTER FOUR

Things went badly at Valdes that winter. Carol was sick with unhappiness, alternating between moods of spiritless despondency and savage efforts to be cheerful. We went out together now and then, but I knew that I could never really take Eon's place. As far as I could, I let the project take hers.

The source of the security leak had never been found. General Barlow decided that it must have been only a thoughtless slip of somebody's tongue, in the wrong company perhaps, but damage enough was already done.

If the commissars were really fishing for more information, they got none. They kept hammering at us with their propaganda barrages until the phrase "pig-headed atomic murderers" began to get under everybody's skin, but the general refused to authorize any official statement that we were not really about to detonate the Earth.

Even in America, the, seed of lies took root. Responsible newspaper and TV reporters picked up the propaganda charges. Carol herself began quizzing me uneasily about how much lithium was dissolved in sea water, and what would keep it from reacting with the hydrogen.

Dr. Draven, the President's stooped old scientific adviser, flew out from Washington with more bad news.

"You'd think the Comrades were falling for their own propaganda." His yellow parchment face was creased with a faint sardonic smile. "They're acting as if they really believe you're about to set atomic fire to the planet."

Apprehension quenched his yellow smile.

"Central Intelligence says they're getting set for what they'll probably call a preventive attack on our main industrial and defense centers. Valdes seems to be Target Number One. Their mobilization schedule doesn't leave you much more time."

We tried to rush the project.

But we were already working under too much pressure. Tired men blundered. A superconductor coil was cooled too fast in the annealing furnace, so that it blew out on the test rack. Dr. Zerlinger was critically burned by the flash of vaporized metal, and without his dogged courage the rest of us found it hard to keep our faith in the *Light Year* alive.

Even the weather was against us. Unpredicted floods of rain turned the desert soil to bottomless mud that sank beneath our test racks on the field. Later in the winter, when that damage had been repaired, unforecast blizzards came howling across the mesa whenever we tried to schedule an open-air test. Spring brought savage southwest winds and abrasive clouds of yellow grit that cut the finish from whatever it touched. A sandstorm was blowing when Carol called me at the shop, late one Sunday afternoon.

"Guess what!" She was breathless with excitement. "Eon's here!"

"I'll keep out of sight." I tried not to seem too sulky. "Just forget our dinner date. I've work enough to do."

"Wait, Charley!" Her voice seemed puzzled and somewhat hurt. "It's you he wants to see. So please come on out. I'm cooking a Mexican dinner for the three of us."

"I don't want to see Eon," I protested. "And I'm afraid it wouldn't be a very cozy party."

"You've got to come." She seemed oddly desperate. "You'll see why."

Eon opened the door for me, at her apartment. The change in him astonished me, not that he had become any sleek and cynical huckster. Though his shirt was clean for once, his dark hair was still rumpled untidily, and his gaunt face looked sullen and hungry as ever. The difference was a new sureness in him, a glint of purpose in his unsmiling eyes and a strength in his quick handshake, which made me wonder what had happened to him.

"Hullo, Guilborn." He took my hat and nodded at a chair, as if he owned the place. "I want to talk to you. About your experiments with the hydro-lithium reaction."

"Hold on, Hunter." I reached for my hat. "You were employed here. You ought to know I can't discuss anything of the sort with any unauthorized person. Certainly not with you."

He kept my hat.

"Take it easy, Guilborn." He grimaced stiffly. "I'm not looking for any more trouble with the FBI. I don't want any secrets. I flew back here just to tell you something."

"Don't tell me." I got hold of my hat. "If you know anything you think ought to be reported, Carol can give you the number of the project security office."

I was turning to leave, when Carol came out of the kitchenette, trailing the tantalizing odors of tacos and enchiladas. She was adorably domestic, with a smudge of flour on her nose, but when I saw the look she gave Eon, I knew she was farther away from me than the moon.

"Charley, you've just got to listen." She took my hat and hung it in the entry closet.

"Okay." I sat down reluctantly facing Eon. "I'll listen. But first I want to know where you've learned anything at all about anybody's research into the hydro-lithium reaction."

"From two sources, Guilborn," he answered quietly. "From the FBI, when you set them after me. From all the recent news stories about the danger of a thermonuclear reaction getting out of control, after the federal men had called them to my attention."

"If that propaganda has upset you, you can start relaxing," I told him. "Of course it's true there is a trace of lithium in sea water, and somewhat more in the crust of the Earth and even in your own body. There's plenty of hydrogen. But the two elements have existed side by side since the Earth was born, through every sort of cataclysm. No conceivable effect could set off an uncontrolled reaction—"

"Wrong, Guilborn," Eon broke in softly. "There's one effect that you have failed to consider."

He spoke with a disconcerting air of knowing what he was talking about. I flinched from a pang of alarm, before I could remind myself that he had always been peculiarly opaque to every fact of science.

"Huh?" I blinked and got my breath. "What effect?"

"It follows from the working of what you might call a metaphysical law. I got the first hint of it years ago, back in high school, when Carol and I fouled up your gravity experiment." He grinned sardonically. "Remember?"

"No experiment works every time," I muttered defensively. "But what is this metaphysical law that is going to blow up the Earth?"

He paused to smile fondly up at Carol, as she came to sit on the arm of his chair.

"This may upset you, Guilborn." He looked back at me, as quietly deliberate as if he had failed to catch my intended sarcasm. "But you'll eventually have to accept the discovery I have made—that nature isn't quite the cold dead machine that you physicists like to imagine."

"Then what is it?"

"Mind and matter are bound together more closely than even the parapsychologists have ever guessed," he said. "I believe the universe was created by Intelligence. I know it responds to creative belief."

"Somebody—Jeans, I think—used to say that the Architect of the universe must have been a mathematician. And I suppose mathematics is a mental exercise." I nodded impatiently. "But what's this about creative belief?"

"The universe is not complete." Eon stood up excitedly. "Creation is still going on." His low voice turned hoarse with a hurried urgency, and his deep-set eyes were burning with something like fanaticism. "Everything around us is still being molded and remolded by what people believe."

I tried not to smile. "So you think we're all suffering from a kind of mass hallucination that the world exists?"

"No." He scowled at my amusement. "The universe is real enough. But it's still evolving. The process is quite orderly and usually very gradual, something that has been going on around us all our lives, so much a part of us that we're seldom aware of it at all—"

"If you're talking about the evolution of life on Earth, or of the stars in the galaxy—"

"I'm not," he said sharply. "I'm talking about more basic changes in what you call the laws of nature."

"The crust of the Earth is a record that goes back a couple of billion years, and it's full of proof that nature hasn't changed very much in that short time."

I couldn't help smiling again. "I guess it's no secret that we're working with the laws of physics here at the project, but I certainly haven't noticed any alterations from day to day."

"You never will." He stalked toward me restlessly. "Because all your laboratories are set up on the false premise that the laws of nature never change. I had to find a different sort of laboratory, to test my theory about that metaphysical law. That's why I went into the advertising game."

"Huh?" I had hardly heard him, because I was busy formulating a new theory of my own. The saturnine defiance smoldering in his eyes and snarling in his voice brought back his old threat that he would adjust the world and not himself, and I recalled that the source of our security leak had never been found. If Eon had been responsible after all, it occurred to me, he must have come back now with this preposterous fabrication to trick me into spilling something more about the project. I decided to play along with him, and report everything to Colonel Fearing.

"And what did you find out?"

"The theory holds up, Guilborn." His dark, hard face wore a cold elation. "If enough people really believe anything, it tends to become the truth!"

"That's too much!" I couldn't help snorting. "Haven't you got the cart in front of the horse? Physical effects do create faith, but I doubt very much that the proposition works the other way around—"

"But it does." Annoyance began to edge his voice. "That metaphysical truth is the very foundation of the universe. Naturally it's hard for you to grasp, because you're a scientist. You're used to thinking backwards. But if you'll open your mind for half a minute, I can show you that everything around us has been shaped by belief."

"You mean the Earth used to be flat, because people thought it was?"

"Exactly!" He nodded triumphantly. "No doubt magic used to work, in prehistoric times, as well as atom bombs do today. The apparent facts of your modern scientific universe were not discovered, Guilborn. They were invented. You've invented some of them yourself."

The sheer novelty of that notion caught me for an instant.

"Just look back at your own work," his urgent voice went on. "Wasn't the experimental evidence always pretty flimsy and ambiguous, in the beginning? Weren't you always pretty anxious to believe you really had something new? Wasn't your main difficulty always to convert the skeptics? Didn't you always have a good many experimental failures—until you had managed to build up a sufficient potential of creative belief to solidify your new idea into fact?"

I shook my head uncomfortably—I couldn't help recalling that first emergency conference in the old resort hotel, when we had shaped the basic theory of the hydro-lithium drive out of nothing more than sheer necessity. Earlier researchers, I remembered, had failed to find any effect at all of magnetic fields upon nuclear cross sections.

But I tried to get hold of myself.

"Nonsense!" I groped wildly for some telling argument. "Suppose magic used to work, as you were saying. What stopped it?"

"Skepticism," Eon answered promptly. "It was a bitter battle of beliefs, fought for several thousand years, with a good many of the champions on both sides burned at the stake. But the scientists, so-called, proved to be the slicker magicians. They finally turned the tide of faith. Their victory uprooted the old facts of magic, and forced their clever new facts into the framework of reality."

"A neat little sophistry." I shrugged. "If I say that the spectra of the distant galaxies prove that the thermonuclear processes have been going on, exactly as we observe them now, for at least half a billion years, you can always answer that my belief has created my proof. But what follows?"

"The end of the world." He looked as grave as if he meant it. "Unless you stop your reckless playing with this hydro-lithium reaction."

"Is that propaganda still eating on you?" I laughed at him for a second or two. "A hundred facts prove there is no possible danger—"

"Perhaps they did," he broke in. "But you have changed the facts."

"How?"

"What you don't realize is that you had to twist the whole universe just slightly out of shape, to create the conditions you need for this reaction." His voice lifted, as I started to protest. "I know what you've done, because I've been following the scientific news from the small nations where knowledge is still free. The good scientists aren't all Americans—and what they report isn't all propaganda! These new reports on the factors involved in the hydro-lithium reaction contradict all the older results. I don't know your mumbo-jumbo, but it's something about phenomenally higher values for the nuclear cross sections, under certain critical conditions—if that means anything."

What that could have meant was something I didn't want to think about. I winced, in spite of myself, from a stab of cold apprehension. But Eon was certainly the world's worst judge of scientific possibilities.

"Plenty of foreign scientists are honestly—and desperately—concerned about the danger that your experiments will start a thermonuclear reaction in the oceans or the crust of the Earth," he rushed on. "You would be, Guilborn, if you weren't shut away here behind your Chinese wall of military security."

His lean face tightened bleakly.

"But I've said my piece," he finished. "The survival of the world depends on what you do about it."

"I'll pass your warning along to Dr. Zerlinger," I said. "You understand that I must report this meeting to the project security officer, too."

He turned white.

"So you still think I'm a spy?"

His bony fists clenched as if he meant to hit me, and Carol ran to grab his arm.

"No, Charley!" She looked at me with tears in her eyes. "You can't mean that!"

I squirmed uneasily in my chair.

"Eon, I don't know what you are." I looked up at his furious, bloodless face, and still I didn't know. "Just a harmless crank, I hope. I still suspect that you ought to see a good psychiatrist. If you were entirely sane, you wouldn't expect me to take any serious stock in this sort of nonsense."

"Then you won't stop that research?"

"Anybody who accepted your ideas would be laughed off the project."

"You poor deluded fool!" Anger grated in his voice. "And I've been just as stupid, wasting my time on you. I see I'll have to do it alone."

He stumbled blindly to the entry closet and came back with my hat. When he saw it wasn't his, he flung it savagely to the floor. Carol caught anxiously at his elbow.

"Darling, please sit down," she begged. "The food is getting cold."

"Food?" He pushed her roughly away. "When your idiot friend is busy blowing up the planet! I've got a plane to catch."

He slammed out.

"I'm so terribly sorry for him." Carol watched him through the window until he was out of sight, and then turned slowly back to me. Her eyes were wet, but she managed not to sob. "Charley," she whispered, "are you really sure he's wrong?"

"Crazy, I'm afraid."

I was picking up my hat, but she made me stay. I thought at first that she was only trying to delay my report to Colonel Fearing, but I liked her too well to care. Perhaps she really wanted me. We ate the Mexican dinner, and drank a fifth of whisky I had brought, and for a little while, with Carol in my arms, I forgot all about Eon.

CHAPTER FIVE

Next day I had a throbbing head, however, and a nagging sense of worry. Eon's metaphysical law still looked like a childish fantasy, but I couldn't forget the way he had somehow sabotaged that high school experiment. At our regular morning conference in the headquarters building, I reported his warning.

"Pure nonsense, of course. But he's so serious about it himself that he almost frightens me. He came all the way out here from New York to warn us. When I failed to take any stock in his weird theory, he threatened to do something on his own—he didn't say what."

"A crank." Zerlinger shrugged.

"Another victim of that propaganda barrage." Colonel Fearing nodded. "It's beginning to crack the civilian morale."

"Softening us up for the bombers." General Barlow cleared his throat explosively. "Intelligence says we're running out of time. Nothing but the *Light Year* can bail us out now. The Pentagon says we've got to have her ready for a test flight, by May first."

"She will be," Zerlinger promised.

"About this Hunter." Barlow swung to Fearing. "Probably just a harmless crackpot. But have an eye on him. Just in case."

The federal agents kept an eye on Eon, and Fearing was soon passing on some pretty strange reports. Eon had not returned to his New York advertising job. He had gone on to Los Angeles instead, and launched a new cult.

"Something he calls the Fellowship of Free Mutationists," Fearing told me. "A weird new religion, I gather, mixed up with a lot of silly hocus-pocus he calls White Magic. He's preaching that people can turn this battered old world into a shining paradise, by faith alone."

"More or less what he was telling me." I nodded. "No doubt he's crazy."

"Crazy like a fox." The colonel smiled. "He used to be an advertising wizard, and he knows how to use every trick in the book to trap the saps. Belief can stop the hell bombs, he keeps preaching, and they're all afraid of hell bombs. They're mobbing him, to stake out their claims in his rosy heaven. Plenty of them have got money to pay for TV time and hook more suckers. Your old friend must be skimming off the millions."

"You're wrong about him," I protested. "Not that I'm defending him. I don't like him. But I'm sure he's more than just a crook. Though I've never felt that I really understood him, I believe he's sincere about this thing. In his own twisted way. That's what worries me. I'm afraid he's crazy enough to do something pretty desperate to keep the *Light Year* on the ground."

"We'll watch him," Fearing promised. "The federal men are already infiltrating his setup, to look for ties with the Kremlin or anything subversive."

THE AGENTS found no foreign ties. The sole inspiration of the Mutationists, they reported, had been Eon Hunter himself. And they said that he was advocating no violent action of any kind. The world was to be rebuilt by faith alone. The only disturbing report was that the investigating agents themselves had begun resigning from the FBI.

"It's got me!" the colonel grumbled uneasily. "They are all trained men, and loyal Americans. They know the desperate crisis we're up against. And still they're quitting. To take up White Magic—whatever that is?"

At the project, all our security precautions were tightened. More barbed wire was strung around the restricted areas, the radar net was spread wider; guided interceptor missiles stood ready for instant flight.

Inside the security screen, we pressed desperately ahead. The spaceframe, as the engineers called the *Light Year's* long hull, was towed out to the testing apron and hauled erect in a tall gantry crane. We installed the big sodium vapor power plant that was to start on chemical fuels and then run on waste energy from the reactor itself. By the middle of April, we were assembling the paramagnetic components and the superconductor coils.

BUSY as we were, however, Dr. Zerlinger gave me a night off, a few days before the date we had set for the test. Eon's new followers were gathering in Albuquerque, and Carol wanted me to drive her there to hear him speak.

The meeting was held in the open air, on the lava-scattered slopes of an extinct volcano west of the city. The size of the crowd amazed me. Though we had arrived two hours before Eon was to appear, we had to park several miles from the hill. We climbed into a murmuring forest of expectant humanity.

It seemed to me at first that Eon's new cult had been rather crudely blended from a mixture of outworn superstitions and the cynical devices of the advertising hucksters. A circle of large stones had been pried upright on the hilltop, like the megaliths of some prehistoric sacred place, and the plume of smoke above them might have come from some Neolithic altar. But the sound trucks cruising about the hillside were new and sleek as the *Light Year*; they were splashed with bright-lettered slogans: BELIEVE AND LIVE! And bawling out recorded music.

The day was windy and raw. We stood shivering on the sharp volcanic rocks, among an odd assortment of neat business men, blanketed Indians, ranchers and miners and farmers, chattering housewives, staring children, uniformed servicemen from the nearby defense installations. A thin Mexican youth came toiling past us on crutches.

"Help me, help me!" he was whining. "Help me touch *El Brujo!*"

"They say he can work miracles." A tall cattleman beside us removed his ten-gallon hat. "Like Christ in the old days!"

The young paralytic stumbled and fell. He lay for a moment whimpering on the rocks, until a plump little man with a white armband came bustling to help him rise.

"Gracias!" he sobbed. "Help me touch *El Brujo!* I wish to walk again!"

"You don't have to touch him," the plump man said. "A true belief is all you need. Wait here, brother, and listen to his message."

The disciple rushed away and the cripple stood leaning on his crutches, waiting with the rest of us in the chilly dusk.

"Believe and live!" a faded old woman was whispering piously. "Believe and live forever!"

"Hogwash!" a small boy jeered at her. "My Dad says Hunter's nothing but a big-mouthed crook—"

"Shut up!" she hissed. "Or he might turn you into a pig."

He gulped and shut up.

"If he can only stop the bombs," a young girl murmured. "That's enough for me."

A breathless silence ran suddenly across the crowd. Another sound truck came lurching toward us down the hill from that circle of standing stones. When it stopped, a man clambered awkwardly into the spotlights on a little platform built over the cab, still so far away that I didn't recognize him.

"Eon!" Carol gasped. "It's Eon!"

The wind had died, and the quiet night seemed suddenly warmer. Eon lifted up his hands in the stillness, and the sound trucks bellowed with his voice. He preached the same fantastic doctrine that I had laughed at that night in Carol's apartment, and the multitudes murmured in awed approval. At the end, he called for a sign in the sky.

"Believe!" The booming of the sound trucks had become almost hypnotic. "Believe that all the evil machines of death must vanish from the Earth, and they will be gone. Believe that better things must come, and your belief will mold them into being. For a sign of the truth, let us create a star!"

He paused dramatically, pointing up into the night. A hundred thousand eyes were lifted to the sky. Carol caught my arm, her fingers quivering with emotion. But for a moment nothing happened.

"A sign!" the sound trucks thundered. "Let us make a shooting star!"

A meteor burned high across the dark.

Somehow, I wasn't much surprised. For one strange moment, as the great gasp of awed adoration swept across the hillside, I even felt a wild elation, as if the faith and will of all those exalted thousands had become a miraculous power in which I could share. A sharp pain caught my throat, and my own tears blurred that fleeting track of light.

I stamped my aching feet and lighted a cigarette, trying to get hold of myself. Canned organ music was rolling out of the sound trucks now, and Eon's tiny-seeming figure stood silent in the spotlights until the eyes of the crowd had come back to him.

"That star is the sign of our new universe!" the sound trucks brayed again. "And all the stars are in our reach! If you want them, follow me. Come now and pledge your faith. We can stop the death machines, and put out the atomic fire that is burning up the Earth, if you will only follow me!"

Carol kissed me suddenly, and tried to slip away.

"Wait!" I stumbled after her and then said, "Don't let him fool you. That meteor was probably just a mass hallucination. Maybe just an accident. It couldn't have been—created!"

She paused, and I caught her trembling arm.

"I'm sorry, Charley. Really terribly sorry." For a moment she clung to me. "It doesn't seem quite fair to you—even if you won't believe. Because you've always been so good to me. But don't you see I must go to him?"

I didn't see, but I had to let her go.

The Mexican boy was struggling up the lava slope again, wailing in the dark because no miracle had healed him. She ran after him, and took his arm to help him. I watched them numbly until they were lost in the mob, and then wandered back unhappily to look for my car.

I drove back to Valdes that night, troubled and alone. Men were still at work around the *Light Year,* when I went by the testing field. In the floodlights, beyond the fences and the guards and the miles of dark mesa, the ship was a white graceful finger pointing toward the stars.

Her shining promise cheered me. She would fly above all interceptors. She would ferry men out to claim and fortify the moon. Even though she carried nucleonic bombs, her cargo would be the Pax Americana. When she had brought peace to all the Earth, she could go on to explore the universe.

And I would be aboard.

Two nights later, we got the last magnet mounted and the last circuit tested and the last gallon of lithium solution pumped into the fuel tanks. Dr. Zerlinger and I came back out from town before three next morning, to recheck everything for the first test flight.

As we turned into the parking area, the headlights of our jeep caught a man crouching against a fin of the ship. I shouted a warning, and the guards were on him in a moment. He stood waiting for them quietly, holding out his empty hands.

"A saboteur?" Zerlinger panted, as we came tumbling out of the jeep. "Or what's he up to?"

"Dunno, sir." A guard clicked handcuffs on the prisoner. "He's got no weapons or explosives, far as I can see. Just a piece of blue chalk."

"That was enough." The prisoner straightened defiantly. "I've grounded your ship."

I recognized his voice.

"Eon!" I gasped. "How'd you get in *here?*"

"Why, hullo, Guilborn." He looked up at me with an un-frightened insolence. "No use trying to tell you how I got inside your stupid barriers. You wouldn't understand."

Zerlinger picked up the piece of blue chalk.

"Huh?" He bent to peer at a ragged star that Eon had scrawled on the bright metal fin. "What's this?"

"A hex mark," Eon said. "I've hexed your ship and everything in it. It will never fly."

"Just a little chalk—" I tried to laugh.

"The chalk itself is nothing," he said. "The pentacle is only an incidental symbol in the rite that I have performed to induce a belief that your wonderful new hydro-lithium drive can't function. Because of that belief, it won't function. And so you won't set the world on fire!"

"We'll soon see what happens," I muttered.

The reactor had to work, because theory was now adequately proven and all our preliminary tests had ultimately been successful—but some vague unease made me turn to scrub the chalk marks off the ship.

Eon laughed behind me.

General Barlow and Colonel Fearing came skidding up in the general's car. The colonel and his men took Eon away to the guardhouse, and the general went aboard the *Light Year* with Zerlinger and me, to oversee the test.

CHAPTER SIX

In half an hour, everything was rechecked and ready for the takeoff. The general climbed into the nose compartment with the pilot. Zerlinger and I strapped ourselves into acceleration seats, down beside the reactor.

A kind of numbness had crept over me, in those last long minutes. All my senses were somehow deadened, and my fingers were clumsy with the straps. Yet I wasn't consciously afraid. There was certainly no reason for fear, I reminded myself—if anything went wrong, if the reaction went out of control, none of us would ever know it. I wondered where Eon had left Carol, and hoped that she would not be involved too painfully when he came to trial. I felt relieved when the general's iron voice began counting off the seconds to takeoff.

"Minus thirty...minus twenty-five..."

At a grunt from Zerlinger, I opened up the idling turbines. They wailed like sirens, gaining speed. The generators whined. The magnetometer needles quivered and shot across their dials, measuring the growing intensity of the reaction field.

"...minus five...minus four..."

Zerlinger pulled a lever, and the fuel pumps began to throb.

"minus one..._take off!_"

I opened the lithium valve and dropped back into the acceleration seat, opening my mouth wide to save my ears from the atomic thunder of the jet. But there was no thunder. I lay there, too numb to breathe, waiting for the atomic drive to hammer us off the Earth, but I felt no thrust.

There was only the purr of the racing generators, and the muffled thrumming of the pumps, and then the sudden harsh rasp of General Barlow's voice on the intercom phone, asking what the hell had happened.

"Nothing." Zerlinger sat up dazedly, mopping at his pale face. "Not even the end of the world!"

We rechecked everything. The magnetometers showed the reaction field at full intensity. The pumps were injecting a full stream of the lithium solution. But there was no nuclear reaction that we could detect, even with a Geiger counter.

"A flat failure!" Zerlinger muttered at last. "I can't imagine why—"

"I can!" rapped the general, who had come down from the nose compartment to watch our frantic search for the trouble. "Come along, and we'll find out…"

We followed him off the *Light Year.* He was shouting for his car, when a jeep came lurching into the floodlights. It screeched to a halt beside us. I saw Colonel Fearing at the wheel. He sat staring at the general, woodenly silent.

"Well, Fearing!" the general barked. "Where's your prisoner?"

"I can't say, sir."

"What's that?"

"I came to report that he's—uh—gone, sir."

"Gone?" The little general stiffened incredulously. "We can't have that. He somehow sabotaged the reactor. I want the truth sweated out of him. That hex business was just an act, to cover up whatever he really did to the ship."

"I don't know, sir."

"You don't know *what?*"

"About that hex business, sir." The colonel cringed from the general's outraged stare. "When we were locking him up, you see, he told me that he was going to hex his way out. We left him alone in a cell, for not more than ten minutes. Guards were watching the corridor outside, all the time. They didn't notice anything. When I came back to interrogate the prisoner, the cell door was still locked. But Hunter wasn't there."

"How'd he get away?"

"I don't know, sir. I searched the cell myself. It appears to be intact. I couldn't get out of it."

"Didn't you find any clue?"

"There was—uh—something, sir. I'm not sure you'll want to call it a clue. But Hunter had found a piece of soap. He had used it to mark a sort of star on the floor of his cell. I don't know why. But I can't help—uh—wondering—"

The air raid sirens interrupted him.

The floodlights flickered once and went off. Fearing bent mechanically to snap off the headlights of his jeep. We stood blind in the unexpected blackout. I tried to hope that it was only an ill-timed practice alert—until a parachute flare blazed overhead, drenching us in a ghastly blue glare.

"The bastards!" General Barlow gasped. "Must have launched their aircraft off submarine carriers! Sneaked in over Mexico—or we'd have picked them up. Caught us with our pants down." His ragged voice lifted. "Take cover men! Wherever you can!"

We staggered off the concrete apron where the dead ship stood, and started digging futile little hollows in the cold desert sand, with only our hands. We were naked.

The whole nation was. The *Light Year* had been our last hope—till Eon came.

Crouching there, I heard a few of our fighters taking off and saw the bright yellow jets of our interceptor missiles rising, but they were nearly all too late. That blue flare kept burning in the sky, and soon I heard the scream of falling bombs.

The enemy, I thought disjointedly, could hardly know that Eon had hexed the project. We were still Target Number One, and the dead hull standing on the apron was the bull's-eye. I buried myself as deep as I could, waiting for the atomic explosions.

The bombs thudded all around us—and somehow I was still alive to hear them. One plunged down so near that it scattered a spray of sand over me, but the only explosion was a great burst of yellow flame from a bomber that crashed a mile south on the mesa.

"Delayed action bombs!" Or maybe only duds!" The man next to me stood up abruptly under that cruel blue light, and I saw that he was General Barlow. "Maybe we've still got a chance!"

He shouted for Colonel Fearing. They ran to the staff car and roared away. As the flare died at last, in the frosty dawn, the bomb disposal squads came out to begin digging gingerly into the new craters around us.

The sirens hooted out the all clear signal. Zerlinger and I climbed shivering out of our shallow pits and limped stiffly back toward the *Light Year*. The tall hull stood untouched—except for the smear of blue chalk on the fin, where I had tried to erase Eon's hex mark—but it had been neatly bracketed by the bombs, and the disposal officer ordered us away.

Numbed from shock and cold, we plodded heavily back across the field toward the shops. I could hear Zerlinger cursing under his breath. We both stopped once to look back at the *Light Year*. She was beautiful in the first glancing sunlight, lean with the atomic might that we had given her to save America, but somehow she was dead.

Colonel Fearing overtook us in a jeep, before we reached the shops. His face was gray and twitching with strain. With only a curt nod at me, he told Zerlinger to get in with him. They went back to where the disposal crews were digging, and I walked on alone.

The mess hall was buzzing with the first wild rumors of the war, when I stopped aimlessly there. The sneak raiders had struck at all our greatest cities and most vital defenses. An H-bomb had blotted out Chicago. Our stockpiles of atomic weapons had all been destroyed on the ground. A Russian space ship had crashed in the Pacific and set off a thermonuclear reaction. The oceans were already boiling. All coastal areas were being evacuated.

Most of that was obvious nonsense—thermonuclear reactions don't stop with boiling water. But I didn't know what to believe. I wandered back to my desk in the shops and waited there, trying to read a paperback novel and listening to each new rumor and longing for something useful to do.

By afternoon, the reports had taken an optimistic turn. Chicago had escaped, after all. Though falling missiles and crashing planes had caused casualties and damage, the enemy atomic weapons had all been duds. Our own air force was hitting back, hard. Moscow had been obliterated. The enemy was already begging for peace.

The facts were stranger than the rumors. I learned them late that night, when General Barlow called me to his office at headquarters. From the bleak set of his jaw, I could see that the war wasn't over, at all. He looked up across his desk with reddened, haggard eyes.

"Well, Guilborn," he snapped. "What do you think of Hunter and his hexes?"

"I don't understand what he could have done to the *Light Year*," I answered uncertainly. But, as a physicist, I can't believe his silly witchcraft did any harm—"

"You may have to," he broke in harshly. "Because I have just received top secret information that Hunter and his gang of traitors have somehow sabotaged our whole stockpile of nuclear weapons."

"Huh!"

"Our strategic aircraft have gone out on retaliatory missions. They are reporting back that all their A-bombs and H-bombs have failed to explode. And now this…"

His hard fingers crumpled a strip of yellow teletype paper.

"Saboteurs have been arrested inside all the secret depots where our nuclear materials are stored. None of these men was caught with any weapons or explosives. Just pieces of chalk. They were scratching what they referred to as hex marks on the doors and walls of the depot buildings. They all admit that they belong to Hunter's crazy cult. They claim they've put the hex on the atom!"

His sick eyes glared at me.

"They succeeded in doing *something*. The officers in charge have begun to make some preliminary investigations. They report that the stored materials still *look* intact. There is no evidence of any tampering—except for those chalk marks. But Geiger counter checks show that the stocks of uranium and plutonium and deuterium have completely lost their radioactivity—"

"Impossible!"

"That's what Zerlinger said, when he heard about it." The general grinned bleakly. "I've sent him over to the nearest depot, to look around for himself."

"My I go—"

"Zerlinger will head the scientific inquiry into how this sabotage was carried out," his brittle voice cut me off. "I've another job for you."

He paused, shuffling papers on his desk without looking down at them. His narrowed eyes studied me, uncomfortable as a surgeon's probe.

"You know the traitor," he rapped at last. "You know his girl. You know, as well as anybody, what he has done to us. I want you to run him down. I'll arrange for you to receive every possible aid. But methods don't matter. Get Hunter!"

CHAPTER SEVEN

I began the search that same night, when Colonel Fearing let me question one of the captured saboteurs. The prisoner was an inoffensive little brown man named Diego Tamayo, who said he owned a curio shop in Santa Fe. There was no evidence that he had any expert knowledge about the handling of nuclear materials—which were dangerous enough, even to experts. But he had been arrested in a natural cavern near Valdes, where a large stock of unassembled components for plutonium bombs had been stored.

"Sure, mister. I'm a Mutationist," he told me. "I joined to save my wife and our baby and the little shop in Santa Fe. And I came to put a hex on the atom bombs in the cave, because Mr. Hunter sent me. I didn't wish to damage government property, because I know the punishments are cruel. But Mr. Hunter said it must be done, to preserve the Earth."

"What equipment did you bring?"

"Nothing." He shrugged, and showed his empty hands. "Except a piece of chalk."

"How did you get inside the cave?"

"With that same chalk."

"I think you're lying," I told him. "But I'll overlook it, if you'll tell me where to find Hunter."

"You will never find Mr. Hunter." Diego Tamayo drew himself up straight. "He has gone to Russia."

"Another lie!" I tried to stare him down. "It's only last night that he escaped from the guardhouse here. The frontiers are all closed. He couldn't have got out of the country."

"I beg your pardon, sir." His mild brown eyes met mine steadily. "It is your misfortune to be mistaken. No frontiers are closed to Mr. Hunter. He can go anywhere he wishes."

"*Any*where?"

"Even to the stars," the curio dealer answered soberly. "With only a piece of chalk."

That was about all we got out of Diego Tamayo, but some of the former federal agents who had joined the Mutationists were still loyal enough to be more helpful. They convinced me that Eon had somehow actually escaped to Russia, but one of them told me that he was coming back to keep a date with Carol Wakeman.

I was waiting when he came.

I had been sworn in as a special agent of the FBI, and trained to shoot an automatic. I was hiding with a county sheriff, in a Kansas cornfield, near a brush-grown pre-historic mound that Eon's followers had used for their queer new rites. Summer had come by then. The war hadn't touched the farm, and a fine stand of growing corn screened us from the unpaved road.

"Listen…" Sheriff Blackacre pressed his leathery ear to the soil. "Here comes your spy…"

For all the fantastic things I had been hearing about Eon's way of travel, it was only a very ordinary gray Ford sedan that came jolting along the road. The driver was the former federal agent who had told us where to wait. He stopped near us just long enough to let Eon out, and then drove on hastily, as if ashamed of what he had done.

Eon waved at him, and waited by the road until the car turned out of sight. He wasn't armed, so far as I could see. Not even with a piece of chalk.

"That him?" The sheriff cocked his worn revolver. He was a stolid old keeper of the peace, with a tobacco-yellowed moustache and only a massive scorn for the newfangled notions of Eon's Mutationists. "Want me to wing him?"

"Not yet," I whispered. "Wait for the girl."

Eon was now striding toward the mound with an air of bright expectancy, as if he expected to find Carol there. But when we stood up in the corn behind him, all I could see was the wide circle of wooden posts that the cultists had set around the crown of the little hill, and the flat stone inside, blackened where they must have burned some ritual fire.

"Ain't no girl," the sheriff muttered. "Nowhere."

"Eon Hunter!" I stepped out of the corn. "We've got a federal warrant for you."

My voice came out too high, and my hands were sweating on the automatic, but Eon turned and grinned almost as if he had been expecting me to hail him.

"Hullo, Guilborn." His grin faded, as he looked at me. "What has happened to you?"

Those last months must had left their mark on me. The Mutationists had stalled the war completely, but how they had done it was still a monstrous mystery. Seemingly, they had somehow sabotaged the whole universe. The Russian nuclear weapons had failed along with our own. The spectral lines of distant stars had shifted, indicating changes in the atomic fires that kept them burning—impossible changes that must have taken place before the light left them, long before Eon was born. Even the luminous dial of my own wristwatch had dimmed, as its trace of radium atoms ceased to disintegrate. I felt that the whole world I knew had crumbled down around me, and Eon must have seen my dazed desperation. But I nodded to the sheriff, and we moved toward him watchfully.

"We'll talk about you," I told him. "And Carol. Where is she?"

"Waiting for me." His dark eyes had a strange sardonic glint. "On the second planet of Altair."

"*What?*"

"Your dead pile of iron, back there at Valdes, wasn't the only road to space. We've found a better one. We've sidetracked all the old problems of fuel and mass and escape velocity that you rocketeers could never really solve. Even the speed of light is no limit now."

I stood gaping speechlessly.

"And I'm on my way to Carol." No longer sardonic, his eyes had lifted toward something far beyond me. "She's waiting on a world I used to dream about, when I was just a boy. A place like the Earth must have been, before it was spoiled with science and machines." He looked abruptly back at me, and his thin face hardened with an old resentment. "But you saw it, when my father showed you my painting of her."

For a moment I could only hate him.

"Are you claiming you can create planets?" I managed to gasp. "Just by thinking them into existence?"

"Not yet." He shook his head regretfully, as if that had been an actual goal. "I doubt that human minds ever can. The truth is less extravagant. It turns out my dreams had been clairvoyant visions. All I had to do was find the planet."

"I really don't know what your game is." My incredulous annoyance was exploding into anger. "But I'm looking for Carol—right here on Earth. If you expect me to believe—"

"I don't," he said. "Because I know you're still convinced that two and two must always equal four. But I can't help feeling sorry for you. You're the same sort of misfit now, that I used to be."

"Never mind that." I tightened my sweaty grasp on the automatic. "But before we let you go riding off into interstellar space on any sort of broomstick, you've got a number of things to explain. First, we want to know how you and your fanatics managed to sabotage our atomic weapons."

"I explained all that a long time ago if you had only understood." He paused to make an odd little gesture at my gun, with his thumb and middle finger formed into a circle. "I didn't like the universe that you physical scientists had hammered together. A lot of other people didn't. So now we've changed it very slightly. If you want me to use your own mumbo-jumbo, we've simply removed the factors of mathematical probability that used to make certain elements unstable."

"How?"

"It's no use, Guilborn." His voice had softened strangely, almost as if with pity. "You won't find any scientific gimmicks. Because there aren't any. All we have done is begin using the spiritual powers of man-powers that you physical scientists always did your best to ignore or deny."

His quickened voice had a ring of awe.

"But they're tremendous, Guilborn! Men like Rhine, and even the older mystics, were only children groping in the dark. Even now, we've just begun to reach the other minds that are re-creating other worlds out through the galaxies. We're still only hoping to work toward communion with the first Mind. That was in the beginning—"

"That's enough mystical bunk!" Perhaps I was afraid to let him go on. "If all you've done is so noble, why did you have to run away to Russia?"

Anger flashed across his face, but then he shrugged tolerantly.

"I didn't run away," he said. "When our work was done in America, I went on to Russia to lead the Mutationist movement there. The materialists in the Kremlin had been as tough to convert as you physicists, but I found enough simple people willing to believe. You'll soon find that the Iron Curtain is being lifted, by liberated men."

"Huh?" I stood blinking at him, half convinced in spite of myself. "I can't understand—"

"You never will, until you unlearn your antiquated ways of thinking. Space and time are different now. You're out of date, Guilborn. Imagine a voodoo priest in your labs at Valdes—back when atomic fusion and fission were still facts of nature."

"But I haven't time to help you now." He glanced restlessly up at that empty circle of posts on the mound. "So long, Guilborn!" He waved his hand, in a hurried little gesture of farewell. "Carol's waiting—"

"Hold on!" I muttered. "We've got to take you back—"

But he was running toward the mound.

"Now?" Sheriff Blackacre leveled his revolver. "Wing him?"

I caught the sheriff's arm. "Let him go."

"Ain't we gonna take him in?"

"No, sheriff." I shook my head painfully; the old ways of thinking weren't easy to unlearn. "Because I guess he's right. He was right, all along. He has been the real hero of everything that happened. I guess I was always the villain. But it's not too late to let him go."

The sheriff holstered his gun reluctantly.

"It's your say-so," he grumbled. "It's no rat-killing of mine."

He stayed behind, but I followed Eon up the mound. My knees were weak, and a cold sweat had come out on my face, but if he had found a new way to reach the stars, I had to see it.

A rock rolled under my foot, on the brushy slope. I stumbled, and lost Eon. When I reached the ring of posts, he was inside. Something was smoldering on the black altar stone, and he was on his knees, scratching with a stick in the dust before it.

I stopped outside the posts, afraid.

Eon stood up, and stepped into the pentacle he had drawn. He was murmuring something I couldn't quite hear. Smoke billowed up from the altar. It filled the circle of posts, and blew out into my eyes. The mound seemed to tremble under me, as if from an earthquake shock.

And the altar stone was gone.

Beyond the row of posts lay another, larger stone. Carol Wakeman was sitting on it, beneath a flowering tree. She wore a lei of flowers, and she was feeding flowers to a fearsome beast that she clearly didn't fear.

"Carol!" Eon was shouting. "Can you hear me?"

She heard him. I saw her luminous smile, as she tossed the flowers to her monstrous pet and jumped up to meet him. Incredibly, across the unimaginable light-years, I heard her joyous voice.

"Darling, darling—"

The smoke was in my eyes again. It swirled away, and left the blackened altar stone where it had been before. Carol and Eon were gone, with all their unknown world. I stood for a long time staring at the pentacle scratched in the dust, before I stumbled back down the mound, to begin trying to learn that two plus two can sometimes equal infinity.

THE END

If you've enjoyed this book, you will not want to miss these terrific titles…

ARMCHAIR SCI-FI, FANTASY, & HORROR DOUBLE NOVELS, $12.95 each

D-1 **THE GALAXY RAIDERS** by William P. McGivern
SPACE STATION #1 by Frank Belknap Long

D-2 **THE PROGRAMMED PEOPLE** by Jack Sharkey
SLAVES OF THE CRYSTAL BRAIN by William Carter Sawtelle

D-3 **YOU'RE ALL ALONE** by Fritz Leiber
THE LIQUID MAN by Bernard C. Gilford

D-4 **CITADEL OF THE STAR LORDS** by Edmund Hamilton
VOYAGE TO ETERNITY by Milton Lesser

D-5 **IRON MEN OF VENUS** by Don Wilcox
THE MAN WITH ABSOLUTE MOTION by Noel Loomis

D-6 **WHO SOWS THE WIND…** by Rog Phillips
THE PUZZLE PLANET by Robert A. W. Lowndes

D-7 **PLANET OF DREAD** by Murray Leinster
TWICE UPON A TIME by Charles L. Fontenay

D-8 **THE TERROR OUT OF SPACE** by Dwight V. Swain
QUEST OF THE GOLDEN APE by Ivar Jorgensen and Adam Chase

D-9 **SECRET OF MARRACOTT DEEP** by Henry Slesar
PAWN OF THE BLACK FLEET by Mark Clifton.

D-10 **BEYOND THE RINGS OF SATURN** by Robert Moore Williams
A MAN OBSESSED by Alan E. Nourse

ARMCHAIR SCIENCE FICTION CLASSICS, $12.95 each

C-1 **THE GREEN MAN**
by Harold M. Sherman

C-2 **A TRACE OF MEMORY**
By Keith Laumer

C-3 **INTO PLUTONIAN DEPTHS**
by Stanton A. Coblentz

ARMCHAIR MASTERS OF SCIENCE FICTION SERIES, $16.95 each

M-1 **MASTERS OF SCIENCE FICTION, Vol. One**
Bryce Walton—"Dark of the Moon" and other tales

M-2 **MASTERS OF SCIENCE FICTION, Vol. Two**
Jerome Bixby: "One Way Street" and other tales

If you've enjoyed this book, you will not want to miss these terrific titles…

ARMCHAIR SCI-FI & HORROR DOUBLE NOVELS, $12.95 each

D-11   **PERIL OF THE STARMEN** by Kris Neville
THE STRANGE INVASION by Murray Leinster

D-12   **THE STAR LORD** by Boyd Ellanby
CAPTIVES OF THE FLAME by Samuel R. Delaney

D-13   **MEN OF THE MORNING STAR** by Edmund Hamilton
PLANET FOR PLUNDER by Hal Clement and Sam Merwin, Jr.

D-14   **ICE CITY OF THE GORGON** by Chester S. Geier and Richard Shaver
WHEN THE WORLD TOTTERED by Lester Del Rey

D-15   **WORLDS WITHOUT END** by Clifford D. Simak
THE LAVENDER VINE OF DEATH by Don Wilcox

D-16   **SHADOW ON THE MOON** by Joe Gibson
ARMAGEDDON EARTH by Geoff St. Reynard

D-17   **THE GIRL WHO LOVED DEATH** by Paul W. Fairman
SLAVE PLANET by Laurence M. Janifer

D-18   **SECOND CHANCE** by J. F. Bone
MISSION TO A DISTANT STAR by Frank Belknap Long

D-19   **THE SYNDIC** by C. M. Kornbluth
FLIGHT TO FOREVER by Poul Anderson

D-20   **SOMEWHERE I'LL FIND YOU** by Milton Lesser
THE TIME ARMADA by Fox B. Holden

ARMCHAIR SCIENCE FICTION CLASSICS, $12.95 each

C-4   **CORPUS EARTHLING**
by Louis Charbonneau

C-5   **THE TIME DISSOLVER**
by Jerry Sohl

C-6   **WEST OF THE SUN**
by Edgar Pangborn

ARMCHAIR SCIENCE FICTION & HORROR GEMS SERIES, $12.95 each

G-1   **SCIENCE FICTION GEMS, Vol. One**
Isaac Asimov and others

G-2   **HORROR GEMS, Vol. One**
Carl Jacobi and others

If you've enjoyed this book, you will not want to miss these terrific titles...

ARMCHAIR SCI-FI, FANTASY, & HORROR DOUBLE NOVELS, $12.95 each

D-21   **EMPIRE OF EVIL** by Robert Arnette
         THE SIGN OF THE TIGER by Alan E. Nourse & J. A. Meyer

D-22   **OPERATION SQUARE PEG** by Frank Belknap Long
         ENCHANTRESS OF VENUS by Leigh Brackett

D-23   **THE LIFE WATCH** by Lester Del Rey
         CREATURES OF THE ABYSS by Murray Leinster

D-24   **LEGION OF LAZARUS** by Edmond Hamilton
         STAR HUNTER by Andre Norton

D-25   **EMPIRE OF WOMEN** by John Fletcher
         ONE OF OUR CITIES IS MISSING by Irving Cox

D-26   **THE WRONG SIDE OF PARADISE** by Raymond F. Jones
         THE INVOLUNTARY IMMORTALS by Rog Phillips

D-27   **EARTH QUARTER** by Damon Knight
         ENVOY TO NEW WORLDS by Keith Laumer

D-28   **SLAVES TO THE METAL HORDE** by Milton Lesser
         HUNTERS OUT OF TIME by Joseph E. Kelleam

D-29   **RX JUPITER SAVE US** by Ward Moore
         BEWARE THE USURPERS by Geoff St. Reynard

D-30   **SECRET OF THE SERPENT** by Don Wilcox
         CRUSADE ACROSS THE VOID by Dwight V. Swain

ARMCHAIR SCIENCE FICTION CLASSICS, $12.95 each

C-7   **THE SHAVER MYSTERY, Book One**
       by Richard S. Shaver

C-8   **THE SHAVER MYSTERY, Book Two**
       by Richard S. Shaver

C-9   **MURDER IN SPACE** by David V. Reed
       by David V. Reed

ARMCHAIR MASTERS OF SCIENCE FICTION SERIES, $16.95 each

M-3   **MASTERS OF SCIENCE FICTION, Vol. Three**
       Robert Sheckley, "The Perfect Woman" and other tales

M-4   **MASTERS OF SCIENCE FICTION, Vol. Four**
       Mack Reynolds, "Stowaway" and other tales

If you've enjoyed this book, you will not want to miss these terrific titles…

ARMCHAIR SCI-FI, FANTASY, & HORROR DOUBLE NOVELS, $12.95 each

D-41   **FULL CYCLE** by Clifford D. Simak
        IT WAS THE DAY OF THE ROBOT by Frank Belknap Long

\
D-42   **THIS CROWDED EARTH** by Robert Bloch
        REIGN OF THE TELEPUPPETS by Daniel Galouye

D-43   **THE CRISPIN AFFAIR** by Jack Sharkey
        THE RED HELL OF JUPITER by Paul Ernst

D-44   **PLANET OF DREAD** by Dwight V. Swain
        WE THE MACHINE by Gerald Vance

D-45   **THE STAR HUNTER** by Edmond Hamilton
        THE ALIEN by Raymond F. Jones

D-46   **WORLD OF IF** by Rog Phillips
        SLAVE RAIDERS FROM MERCURY by Don Wilcox

D-47   **THE ULTIMATE PERIL** by Robert Abernathy
        PLANET OF SHAME by Bruce Elliot

D-48   **THE FLYING EYES** by J. Hunter Holly
        SOME FABULOUS YONDER by Phillip Jose Farmer

D-49   **THE COSMIC BUNGLARS** by Geoff St. Reynard
        THE BUTTONED SKY by Geoff St. Reynard

D-50   **TYRANTS OF TIME** by Milton Lesser
        PARIAH PLANET by Murray Leinster

ARMCHAIR SCIENCE FICTION CLASSICS, $12.95 each

C-13   **SUNKEN WORLD**
        by Stanton A. Coblentz

C-14   **THE LAST VIAL**
        by Sam McClatchie, M. D.

C-15   **WE WHO SURVIVED (THE FIFTH ICE AGE)**
        by Sterling Noel

ARMCHAIR MASTERS OF SCIENCE FICTION SERIES, $16.95 each

MS-5   **MASTERS OF SCIENCE FICTION, Vol. Five**
        Winston K. Marks—Test Colony and other tales

MS-6   **MASTERS OF SCIENCE FICTION, Vol. Six**
        Fritz Leiber—Deadly Moon and other tales

If you've enjoyed this book, you will not want to miss these terrific titles…

ARMCHAIR SCI-FI & HORROR DOUBLE NOVELS, $12.95 each

D-51 **A GOD NAMED SMITH** by Henry Slesar
       WORLDS OF THE IMPERIUM by Keith Laumer

D-52 **CRAIG'S BOOK** by Don Wilcox
       EDGE OF THE KNIFE by H. Beam Piper

D-53 **THE SHINING CITY** by Rena M. Vale
       THE RED PLANET by Russ Winterbotham

D-54 **THE MAN WHO LIVED TWICE** by Rog Phillips
       VALLEY OF THE CROEN by Lee Tarbell

D-55 **OPERATION DISASTER** by Milton Lesser
       LAND OF THE DAMNED by Berkeley Livingston

D-56 **CAPTIVE OF THE CENTAURIANESS** by Poul Anderson
       A PRINCESS OF MARS by Edgar Rice Burroughs

D-57 **THE NON-STATISTICAL MAN** by Raymond F. Jones
       MISSION FROM MARS by Rick Conroy

D-58 **INTRUDERS FROM THE STARS** by Ross Rocklynne
       FLIGHT OF THE STARLING by Chester S. Geier

D-59 **COSMIC SABOTEUR** by Frank M. Robinson
       LOOK TO THE STARS by Willard Hawkins

D-60 **THE MOON IS HELL!** by John W. Campbell, Jr.
       THE GREEN WORLD by Hal Clement

ARMCHAIR SCIENCE FICTION CLASSICS, $12.95 each

C-16 **THE SHAVER MYSTERY, Book Three**
       by Richard S. Shaver

C-17 **THE PLANET STRAPPERS**
       by Raymond Z. Gallun

C-18 **THE FOURTH "R"**
       by George O. Smith

ARMCHAIR SCIENCE FICTION & HORROR GEMS SERIES, $12.95 each

G-5 **SCIENCE FICTION GEMS, Vol. Three**
      C. M. Kornbluth and others

G-6 **HORROR GEMS, Vol. Three**
      August Derleth and others

If you've enjoyed this book, you will not want to miss these terrific titles…

ARMCHAIR SCI-FI & HORROR DOUBLE NOVELS, $12.95 each

D-61 **THE MAN WHO STOPPED AT NOTHING** by Paul W. Fairman
TEN FROM INFINITY by Ivar Jorgensen

D-62 **WORLDS WITHIN** by Rog Phillips
THE SLAVE by C.M. Kornbluth

D-63 **SECRET OF THE BLACK PLANET** by Milton Lesser
THE OUTCASTS OF SOLAR III by Emmett McDowell

D-64 **WEB OF THE WORLDS** by Harry Harrison and Katherine MacLean
RULE GOLDEN by Damon Knight

D-65 **TEN TO THE STARS** by Raymond Z. Gallun
THE CONQUERORS by David H. Keller, M. D.

D-66 **THE HORDE FROM INFINITY** by Dwight V. Swain
THE DAY THE EARTH FROZE by Gerald Hatch

D-67 **THE WAR OF THE WORLDS** by H. G. Wells
THE TIME MACHINE by H. G. Wells

D-68 **STARCOMBERS** by Edmond Hamilton
THE YEAR WHEN STARDUST FELL by Raymond F. Jones

D-69 **HOCUS-POCUS UNIVERSE** by Jack Williamson
QUEEN OF THE PANTHER WORLD by Berkeley Livingston

D-70 **BATTERING RAMS OF SPACE** by Don Wilcox
DOOMSDAY WING by George H. Smith

ARMCHAIR SCIENCE FICTION & FANTASY CLASSICS, $12.95 each

C-19 **EMPIRE OF JEGGA**
by David V. Reed

C-20 **THE TOMORROW PEOPLE**
by Judith Merril

C-21 **THE MAN FROM YESTERDAY**
by Howard Browne as by Lee Francis

C-22 **THE TIME TRADERS**
by Andre Norton

C-23 **ISLANDS OF SPACE**
by John W. Campbell

C-24 **THE GALAXY PRIMES**
by E. E. "Doc" Smith

IT ALL STARTED AT THE ZOO...

How in the world does a writer for Raymond A. Palmer's "Fantastic Adventures" magazine end up in a far-off world filled with beautiful Amazon women, giant black panthers, sword-wielding savages, and bloodthirsty dragons? It sounds a bit crazy, but that's what happened to Berkeley Livingston, who was pulled into a strange world where all men bowed their heads in fear of the great Queen Luria...

It began innocently enough with a trip to the zoo. However, upon entering the cat house, Livingston and Hank Sharpe found themselves face to face with the most remarkable Panther any man had ever laid eyes upon. Soon after, both men found themselves falling through into another dimension—into a world torn by violence, war, and intrigue.

CAST OF CHARACTERS

BERKELEY LIVINGSTON
Roy Rogers got to play himself in nearly all of his movies. Why not the same for a pulp magazine writer?

HANK SHARPE
This small guy with incredibly strong hands heard a calling from another world and so he went there—the land of eternal mists.

LURIA
A queen from another world—she was a black-haired beauty whose mode of transportation was black, fast, and very unique.

LOKO
It didn't matter if the whole world crumbled around him, so long as he could gain enough power to control it.

LOVAH
In regular clothes she could pass for any average girl on the street, but she did pack one helluva punch.

MOKAH
On the surface he was just a black panther, but an incredibly big black panther with nearly human intelligence.

CAPTAIN MITA
He was a big brute, and one of Loko's top henchmen, but he wasn't really as strong as he looked.

QUEEN OF THE PANTHER WORLD

By
BERKELEY LIVINGSTON

ARMCHAIR FICTION
PO Box 4369, Medford, Oregon   97501-0168

The original text of this novel was first published by Ziff-Davis Publishing Co.

Armchair Edition, Copyright 2012, by Gregory J. Luce
All Rights Reserved

For more information about Armchair Books and products, visit our website at…

www.armchairfiction.com

Or email us at…

armchairfiction@yahoo.com

CHAPTER ONE

I DO NOT say that adventure cannot begin anywhere. Of course it can! And usually does. But let us speak of *specific* places. I once met a Metropolitan baritone singing in a cheap honky-tonk on west Madison Street. He said it was the only place he knew of where he could act as he wished, drink what he wanted, and talk to the people he wanted. And fight with whom he pleased. Turned out he had once planned on being a fighter until some rich woman heard him sing...

I was once a skip-tracer for a collection outfit and followed a man all the way to Mexico City; he owed a certain merchant fifty thousand dollars and had the money. And while I was trying to locate this skip, the police of Mexico City thought I was an international agent and dogged my steps until one night they thought they had something on me and clapped me in the calaboose and held me incommunicado for twenty-four hours before I could get in touch with the consulate...

But let me be even more specific.

It began on a wondrous spring day.

Summer was not quite ready to thrust its heat against us, the air was warm and fragrant with growing things, I had a couple of bucks in my kick and I had just fallen out of love. I believe I said it was a wonderful day...? Well, I'd called Henry Sharpe the night before and we had made plans to go to Brookfield Zoo where the animals can come up close and sneer at the humans.

"A weekday's best," Sharpe said as I slid into the seat beside him. "Sunday brings out the weekend nature lover and his camera. Besides, the animals aren't quite so bored on a weekday. Maybe…"

"Maybe what?" I asked. I wasn't looking at him but was watching him get out into the traffic of La Salle Street.

"Nothing," he said shortly. He was looking straight ahead but there was an odd crinkle to his forehead as though he was thinking of something that bothered him.

*　　*　　*

We parked and began the long walk to the animal houses. As Hank had predicted, there weren't many people about. I saw a group of school children herded by their teacher moving determinedly toward the aviary. But our paths did not converge. Sharpe is the fastest walking little man I've ever known. I'm not on the big side myself and it's always been a problem keeping up with him unless I go at a half-trot. After some few hundred yards, I was getting a bit winded.

"Hey! Take it easy. We got all day," I said, panting heavily.

"Sorry, Berk," he said. "But it's such a relief getting away from those damn drawings… Besides, I'm anxious to see something."

"So am I," I said. "But at the rate we're moving I'll need a chair to see them in. I'm that pooped."

We slowed after a while to a more sedate run. By that time I'd given up the struggle and was dragging my tail ten feet behind Sharpe. I had been so busy just keeping pace with him I hadn't even noticed where he had made his goal. I leaned my weight over the iron rail and looked across the moat to where the animals lolled in the sun. The scene was a rocky bit of jungle land. There were painted limitations of rocks, bushes, trees, and a small grotto led to the inside cages. There were some four of them there, great black things, panthers all; mama, papa and a couple of baby panthers, which didn't look any different than their parents. At least their teeth were no smaller when they yawned.

ONE OF them rose and strolled to the edge of the moat and fell to his haunches and stared at us out of his great yellow eyes. There's something about the big cats, lions, tigers, panthers, the whole feline tribe, down to the smallest tabby, that reaches right down and pulls at the atavistic remembrances of man. I felt the hair rise at the nape and knew my breath was catching as the beast looked at the two of us. It was as though I could reach through the bone and fur to that tiny brain and pluck out what lay there. It was as if he was saying, five minutes out there and we'd see who'd be boss.

"That's right, baby," I said aloud. "But you're in there and I'm out here…"

"Huh?" Hank whirled to me.

I grinned and told him what I'd been thinking of. But the grin was wiped from my lips at what I saw in his eyes. They were just wild in excitement.

"So you heard it too," he said.

"Heard what?" I asked.

"What the panther said."

"Now *wait* a minute. I didn't hear *anything!* A picture formed in my mind of what the beast might be thinking if he could think."

He turned back then and looked at the beast. I saw that his fingers were white against the rail. I saw too that the knuckles were bloodless. Something was wrong. I puzzled over it then turned my attention to another of the tribe. This one I hadn't seen before. He was coming out of the semi-darkness of the grotto into the sunlight. I gasped at the size of him. He was the biggest panther I'd ever seen, a full seven feet from head to tail-tip. He stalked out into the sunlight and stood poised, the only movement a sinuous twitch of the black tail. I don't know how the beast at the lip of the moat heard or knew of the other's presence, but before our amazed eyes, it turned and leaped toward the other with a blood-chilling scream of anger.

I heard Hank's sibilant intake of breath, heard the muted, "Aah!" that came from his lips. But my whole attention was taken by the drama before us.

The giant panther waited the coming of the smaller one with the utmost equanimity. It didn't do any more than face the other. Not even its tail twitched. Yet when the smaller one was but a few paces away, in fact the other had already leaped in a wild lunge, then the big beast moved. But when it moved it was a greased streak of black lightning. I have never seen anything move so fast. One second it was facing its adversary, the next it had reared and slashed at the bundle of charged dynamite which had flung itself at him. There was but a single blow. There must have been terrific power in that paw to do what it did. For the smaller beast was flung a good five yards through the air. It landed heavily on its back, rolled over and began to drag itself toward the other. I saw then that its back had been broken by the blow. I let a whistle escape my lips.

There was more to come. As though the smaller one's leap had been a signal, all the others converged on the single monstrous thing in the center of the arena. Only this time the immense beast did not wait for the attack. It leaped like a bolt straight for the largest of its enemies. I didn't know that the big cats felt or knew fear. At least not till then. But as the huge thing left its feet, the smaller one turned and leaped screaming for the protection of the grotto. And behind it came the others. I turned quickly to the remaining one. It stood facing the grotto mouth after it landed. There was a snarl on its mouth and the huge canines turned me cold inside.

I COULDN'T take my eyes from the monster. It moved so slowly, so premeditatively. I watched it move toward the maimed panther, which had stopped its futile movement and lay stretched full length on the ground. The big one approached the other at an angle. When it was only a few feet away it swerved and came in from the rear. The beast on the ground must have had an intuitive idea why because it tried to turn to face the enemy. Before it could complete the turn the big one was on him. It was over quickly. A single, bone-crunching snap of the huge jaws and life departed for the broken-backed panther. It was then the keepers appeared.

A shuddering sigh was wrenched from Hank's lips as the keepers busied themselves with fire hoses, used, I supposed for just such an emergency. The powerful streams of water hit the panther from three sides and drove him snarling backward to the grotto. When it finally disappeared into it a gate was lowered. I wanted to stay and see what happened then. But Hank had other ideas.

"No. I've seen enough," he said. "Besides, I've got something to tell you."

We didn't go far, only to the place where the elephants stood, great brown splotches against the deeper brown of their surroundings. Hank made sure we were removed from the rest of the crowd before he began to talk.

"Berk, do you think I'm goofy?" he asked.

"The goofiest guy I know," I said with a laugh. "I've always said that…"

He should have smiled. He should have done anything but what he did, grab my wrist and pull me closer to him.

"Wait!" he said sharply. "I'm not kidding. Let me start from the beginning because that way I'll get things in order.

"In the first place you know the kind of guy I am about animals. Always traipsing off somewhere, to the Forest Preserve, or the dunes or, some zoo or other. Just because I like to see the animals, the big ones and the little ones. I've always been interested in them, as if there was a bond between us. You've often mentioned that I'm the only guy you know who can walk up to a cat, for instance and immediately it'll start purring. Or to a dog, no matter how big, and it'll eat out of my hand. Well, something strange happened last week. Brookfield opened then for the summer. Of course I was one of the first to get here.

"Well, through the years I've become pretty well-known out here and they let me have my run of the place. So the first thing happens, Joe Edson, the head keeper grabs me and drags me up to the big cathouse. Takes me up to the panther cage and says:

" 'Look, Hank.' "

"Look at what?" I asked.

" 'The size of that cat.' "

"Berk, it was the biggest cat I've ever seen. Now get this. Panthers are the smallest of the big cats. They're really small lions. But this baby, the same one we just saw was bigger than even the biggest lion. But it was a panther. It was a panther but for one thing, its canines. They were those of a tiger. Bigger, longer, Berk, than any tiger's."

I was following him pretty good. So far he hadn't said anything to warrant the state of excitement he was in. But I hadn't heard everything.

He went on:

"Ed got a call from one of the keepers just then and I was left alone. The cat was in a far corner. Soon as Ed left, the cat got up and moved close to the bars and faced me. He looked at me with those devil's eyes of his and his lips parted in a grin. Damn! It was almost human, that grin. I wondered where they got such a magnificent animal... Berk! I swear to God, this is what happened. The cat said, 'You wouldn't believe it if it were told to you.' "

I KNOW I was smiling when Hank said what he did. And I know the smile was still on my face as I turned and looked him full in the eyes. But a cold rope dragged itself down my spine and suddenly my hands felt clammy with sweat. He must have seen something of what went on in my mind because he went on quickly:

"Yeah! Sounds goofy. Really insane. But true. As I stand here with you, it's the truth. And there's even more. I guess I just stared at the damned cat. Suddenly it moved back and forth against the bars in that sinuous walk only cats have. After a few turns it came back and faced me again. It was just as though its mind was troubled and the turns it took enabled it to clear its mind for what it wanted to say. '*She* brought me here to prove something. But now I'm in this prison and only *she* can get me out. You must help me...'

"There were words trembling on my lips but they simply wouldn't pass. I was speechless. Yet he read my mind. For he answered the words that had formed in me. 'You are the only person on this planet who can help me. Project your thoughts into the great void. Call, *Luria*... And when the answer comes, say that Mokar believes...'

"I guess I was in a sort of mental fog for a while after that because the next remembrance was of my studio. I sort of came out of the trance I was in and found myself on the couch. I know that I had left the zoo and driven back to the studio; I must have! Anyway, the first thought in my mind was what Mokar had said. I did it..."

"Did what, Hank?" I breathed softly.

"Called to this Luria."

"And...?"

"She not only answered, she came to me. Not in flesh," he hastily assured me. "It was a sort of picture I got of her. Oh, man! What a picture though. I deal in beauty. Now and then we run across some beautiful models. But this Luria... Out of this world is the only way to describe her. Her skin was white as the proverbial snow and yet it had an odd pinkish glow to it. Her hair was midnight and it sparkled as though a million snowflakes were reflecting light from it. She wore a breastplate, which concealed her charms yet barely covered her swelling flesh so that my breath was taken from me. Below the plate she was bare to her loins, which again was covered by a leather belt from which dangled a jeweled dagger. In her hand, the right one, she carried a spear with an immense blade, slim, and murderous looking.

"She was clothed in mist which swirled and eddied about her. Because of this strange mist the picture was none too clear except in glimpses. But the oddest part of the whole scene was a *something* that lurked in the background. Lurked is the only word for it. It was never clear at all. I got the feeling of a long body, wetly metallic-looking and covered by a serrated series of spines. But as I say, I'm not sure. Maybe that was the proof of my hallucinated state."

I released my breath in a sigh and said:

"The wrong one of us is writing. I'd say this dame brought out the poet in you, Hank. Never have I heard a woman described like this. Now look..."

"I was sober. More sober than at any time of my life," he said, as though he knew what I was going to say. "But let me finish. The message of Mokar came to my mind and I saw her lips smile. They formed words and across the misty dimness came the answer, "Tell Mokar I shall come for him soon." He hesitated for an instant, opened and closed his mouth and finally said nothing.

"And that's the last you've ever heard of or seen the beautiful dream gal, Luria?" I said.

He shook his head, yes.

I DIDN'T know what to say. Hank Sharpe was my dearest friend. He was a mixture of the strangest things, for at one and the same time he was the most hardheaded, clear-thinking man I'd ever known; and at the same time the world's greatest romanticist. He spoke of the evil of man with a knowing look. Yet he could not believe evil of anyone. He was as small as I and even thinner, and no one has ever called me, big-boy, but he was as strong as a horse with hands that were like a carpenter's, tough and muscular. I've seen him slap a guy and send the guy all the way across a tavern floor with that slap. He had a head that was a bit too large for the rest of him, with a face that was long and lean and handsome. And there was nothing I wouldn't do for the guy... But this deal he was talking of sounded like a hashish dream.

It couldn't be, though.

There might be a way of finding out, I thought. "Look, Hank," I said. "Let's mosey over to the cat house. I want to see something."

There was quite a crowd on the outside. Evidently the word of the fight had spread and they had gathered to see what there was to be seen. There wasn't much. What blood had flowed had been washed clean by the hoses. Of the cats nothing was to be seen. We strolled around and walked into the huge place. It was apparent which cage the panthers were in by the crowd watching. We joined the others.

Being on the small side we edged our way through the crowd until we stood against the iron railing which separated the cages from the spectators. The animals in the cage were restless. Whether it was the fight which had made them so or something else, they paced back and forth, growls rumbling deep in their throats and sometimes coming past the furry pockets. Oddly enough, the largest and most ferocious, the huge jet-black beast whose name was Mokar, was the least restive. He lolled at his ease on the shelf, which they used for resting and sleeping.

He was lying there until he spotted us. Then with an immense and effortless leap he was at the bars, his great yellow eyes searching our faces. Suddenly it happened. I swear Mokar smiled. Those fearsome lips parted in a huge cat's grin.

And Hank turned to me and said:

"Let's go. He understood."

It was just too much for me. I shook my head and started to follow Hank. But I hadn't done more than make a half-turn when he gripped my forearm so hard I *yipped* in pain.

"It's her," he whispered in a voice of awe.

Like a flash I followed the direction of his eyes and beheld her. I *knew* it was her. Yet she was like night and day as far as accuracy of description. Only in the small wave of hair which peeked beneath the hood of her coat was there something of what he'd described, the hair whose blackness held the sheen of a million reflected snowflakes. Her skin too was as he said. But that face! It was the face of a million men's dreams. So alluring, so innocent, eyes that begged for love, and knew only virtue, lips whose redness made one hungry for their touch, and a skin that was like a flower petal. I felt my fingers contract in a spasm, as though they had a will to fly toward that loveliness for a caress.

"Your friend likes me," the girl said.

She had spoken and in perfectly understandable English.

"I'm glad," she went on. "Mokar will be too."

"He will?" I said.

"But of course. He has learned his lesson and I have found what I looked for. Now we will go out of this place of prison in to the clean air. Come!"

IT WAS a command. And we followed. She led us directly to one of the open-air confectionery stands. She walked up and ordered an ice cream cone. I reached for the dime automatically. But Hank ordered two more and paid for them. She turned and walked to a bench close by. We followed as if we were tied to her by a string. So we sat, the three of us, munching on our cones until the last of them were licked up. All the while she sat and stared at anything and everything but us.

She sighed breathless after a while and still looking straight ahead, said:

"It is good not to be alone. Poor Mokar. He missed me and could not get through the valley of the mists to me. Luckily he found you, my friend."

Hank is a slow-acting guy most of the time. Then again he acts with the speed of a fighter throwing a counter punch. This was one of those times. Suddenly his hands imprisoned hers and he was facing her.

"Uh, huh," Hank said. "That's right. He found me and you found me. So that makes everything just right. But where does it leave me?"

She was innocence itself. "How do you mean?"

"Who are you? Where do you come from? What's this all about, this business with Mokar; how did you manage to hypnotize me into the dream I had?" Hank shook her hands imprisoned in his for emphasis.

She didn't answer immediately but looked down at her hands, which were beginning to show a redness from the tightness of his grip. Hank flushed and released her hands.

She threw back her head in an odd gesture and the hood fell away from those beautiful tresses, which fell in a wonderfully effective wave about her shoulders. Even I, who can take my women or leave them alone, felt a thrill at the sight.

"I am Luria," she said. "You know that. And I come from the valley of the mists…"

"You come in dreams," Hank said. "In dreams of mist and terror."

I gaped at the man. What the heck had gotten into him? He had turned so that his profile was to us. This time it was she who took the initiative. She took hold of his hands and began to talk:

"I came to you across the great void. It was hard for I was already here and I had to transpose my soul-self back to the place from whence I'd come. There is no other but you who can understand me. Yet we live side by side. Our worlds are the same. The same in the same time. Will you come back with me and live in this side-by-side world? The time has come when I have need of you…"

"Wait a minute, Hank!" I broke in before he could give this girl an answer. "Don't listen to her. It's some sort of gimmick she's got that's working you. I don't trust her."

"I do, Berk," he said. "I know she's in trouble. I guess I knew it from the beginning. And I want you to come along with us."

"Oh boy!" I chortled in simulated glee. "Ain't that going to be just ducky. Come on along and play, he says. And how do we do that? Hold hands across a table while the lights are out and wait for the *message?*"

"You're not scared, are you?" he asked.

"Now we're playing kid games," I said. *"I dare you…"*

HE TURNED again so that he was facing her. "Is it possible to bring my friend along?"

She nodded. The wrinkle went out of his forehead and a smile lighted his face. He got up and stepped in front of me.

"Well?" he asked.

"Well what?" I was mad. Yet at the same time I felt a thrill of excitement. *If,* I thought, if such a thing could be, why I could write of it later. Fame and fortune could be waiting for me at the end of the trail. But what the heck were we dreaming of? The whole thing was a lot of talk. Dream stuff and coincidence. I snorted loudly. Hank turned back to her and said:

"See. It's my personal charm. He can't resist it. It's because I smoke Regents. They give off that wonderful aroma and make me nonchalant. Also an outcast. Berk smells that way naturally."

"Mokar will be glad," she says. "He likes your friend."

"Yeah?" I said, quick-like. "Well, I like him too. Just where he's at, behind bars."

"Oh," she said just as quickly. "He won't be for very long. When you get to know him better you'll grow much more fond of him. He's so affectionate."

"Then he and Hank'll get along swell. Hank's an animal lover. Now why couldn't he have been crazy about fish? I've always been wild about mermaids," I said.

Hank hummed a bit about, "wild about Nellie." I was too far from him to get in a kick at his shins. Suddenly she rose. It was a movement that was as lithe and sinuous as an animal's. Her fingers threw the hood back around her hair. Hank started to join her but she shook her head.

"No. I must go alone…" she said.

"But how…?"

She knew what he meant. "I will come to you when the time comes," she said. "Nor will it be long."

I covered a grin. Now she was cooking with butane. So she was going to come when the time was ripe. I figured we'd better not hold our breaths that long. We'd probably be ripe too.

But Hank was all trust and hope. He acted like a kid with the promise of a day at the circus before him. His eyes were shining in anticipation of the day. Man alive! You'd think he was ten instead of thirty. His eyes followed her trim, but very trim, figure until it disappeared into the big cathouse.

"Okay kid," I said. "You can wake up. Dream's over."

His lips were bent in a crooked grin but his eyes were dark in some inner thought that was extremely pleasant.

"…Not yet," he said after a moment.

CHAPTER TWO

IT WAS some day in the week, I think Tuesday; at any rate it wasn't long after our visit to the zoo that I got a phone call from Hank. I was busy on a fantasy for *Fantastic Adventures* magazine that had to do with flying disks and I wanted to get some of the facts in order. I had a fistful of clippings on my desk, a cigarette burning itself to death in the ashtray, and a brow full of wrinkles on my forehead. The phone at my side rang and I cussed it as I lifted it from the cradle.

"Yeah…"

"Berk!" Hank's voice crackled in excitement. "Come on over. But fast!"

Oh fine, I thought. He's been dreaming again. Then another thought pierced me through. Maybe…?

"You mean…?" I began.

"Right. Drop what you're doing and shoot out here."

"But look," I began. There was no need to go on, unless I wanted to talk to myself. He'd hung up. Believe me I was in just that mood, talking to myself, I mean. The disk story had to be on the editor's desk by Friday. And I had a good six thousand words to do on it yet. The air was blue with nasty words as I shoved the chair away from the desk and put the old money-machine away. Now why did Hank have to dream, I thought as I put on a pair of slacks! I work in shorts and nothing else. A tee shirt followed the slacks and then socks and shoes. I gave the desk a look of regret as I turned for a last look before closing the door. It was going to be a long time before I saw that desk or room again.

Hank shared a loft studio on north State Street with a couple of other artists. He was alone, sitting before his work desk. There was a half-finished pen and ink drawing on the board. He heard my clattering steps on the rickety stairs and met me at the door. He grabbed my wrist and dragged me into his part of the studio.

"Last night," he began without preamble. "She came to me. She said she would see me again this afternoon. She was in trouble. I saw it in her face. I've got to help her. Berk, *we've* got to help her."

I tried to throw some cold water on him. The whole deal had lost its appeal to me. What the heck! I had this story to do for the boss and besides... I found a seat among the magazines on a chair and said:

"Now listen to me, Hank. I'm serious. I went along with this dream-book stuff you gave me because I thought it was some kind of a gag. I didn't know it was serious. But if it is, you'd better see a psychiatrist. Hallucinations may be all right until they reach the stage where a man can't tell them from reality.

"I guess it's time we talked this thing over seriously. I don't know how it began but I can hazard a guess. I'll bet you went to a party with some of those wacky friends of yours and there was a hypnotist there. And so the gag was for him to use you as a guinea pig. I'll bet there was this gal we met, at the party. The idea being to see how far post-hypnotism would work. I've got to hand it to the lad who did the hypnotizing. He did an A-1 job."

"Uh uh," Hank said. "You're wrong. You're..."

We both noticed it at the same time. All of a sudden there was a terrific breeze in the room. I started to close the window, only I didn't make it. It was as if someone had glued me to the chair I was in. I could see, hear, smell, reason, but couldn't act. I was aware of what was going on only I seemed not to be part of it.

I say there was a great gust of blowing in the room. Yet not a paper stirred, not a leaf in the magazines turned. In fact not a material thing felt the wind's effect except Hank and myself. I saw his hair blowing about his face, saw his shirt collar flap against his chin and knew the same thing was happening to me. I was turned three-quarters to the window and though I couldn't turn completely I saw that not a leaf stirred on a tree directly outside the window. Not a bit of dust blew. And I even saw a man mop his brow below us. The wind increased and with it came a cloud of darkness. It's the only way I can describe it. It was a mist of inky blackness and it flowed up from out of nowhere. I tried to move out of its path. I could feel my muscles strain as I did my utmost to lift myself from its path as it rolled toward Hank and me. But though the sweat stood out on my forehead in huge damp drops and rolled down my arms and chest, all my efforts were unavailing. The black curtain enveloped us. It not only encircled us so that nothing was to be seen beyond it, it also did something to our minds. For suddenly all was darkness.

THERE was a dull feeling at the back of my head. And my neck felt stiff. I opened my eyes and looked blankly about me. We were both still sitting as we had been. Hank looked asleep. I shook my head and instantly realized the spell or whatever it was, was gone.

"Hey! Hank! Wake up fella."

As I called to him I rose from my chair. I groaned aloud as every bone in my body ached with the effort. My words seemed to have no effect. I staggered a bit in the few feet which separated us. My hand had little life in it as it shook him weakly. But it was enough. His eyes opened and looked dazedly about him. Then they began to focus and reason returned to their depths. The old grin appeared on them and he said:

"Well? What do you say now?"

I blew out my breath and sighed. Was nothing going to convince him? But of course. All he had to do was see the outside. I whirled and pointing through the glass, said:

"Lo-oo-yeow!"

The last was a screech of horror. This wasn't State Street. This wasn't Chicago. This wasn't anything I'd ever seen. This was Hell!

We were no longer three flights up. We were at ground level. And what ground. It looked like some cataclysm of nature had ripped and twisted the ground in a mad convulsion. It was bare of foliage and brown and hard with huge boulders strewn about as if giants had been rolling them in a game of bowling. We seemed to be in a sort of hollow, like the bottom of a soup plate. I couldn't see what lay beyond the lip. Hank must have seen the terror and bewilderment in my eyes. He rose and stepped to my side.

"Holy cats..." he breathed softly.

"I could think of other things," I said. "All appropriate to the landscape."

"Save it," he said sharply. "Let's take a look around."

Too anxious I wasn't to see what there was to be seen. But I wouldn't have stayed alone for all the tea in China. Matter of fact I hoped we *were* in China. But at the pit of my stomach was a feeling that we weren't in China. It was the kind of feeling that said, brother, you're in the next place to where you've always said you're going.

If Hank had any fears they were well concealed. He moved along, head up and shoulders back like he knew exactly where he was going. My steps lagged but only a few yards behind his. We climbed the few feet to the lip of the earthen bowl and looked about. I know my mouth hung open and that to anyone who might have been looking on I played the part of an idiot very well. At least I had company.

THE ground fell away below our feet steeply for a distance of perhaps a thousand feet. Below us lay a sight to gladden the heart of any farmer. The ground was checkerboarded in neat patterns that sometimes were squares and sometimes rectangles and sometimes even triangles of color. There were trees, heavy-planted like parklands, and we could see areas that looked dark with luxurious growth. The air was warm and fragrant and peaceful. It was a placid scene.

But only for a moment.

Immediately below us the ground was sheer. But to either side the slope was gradual. Suddenly there was a great snorting chorus of animal sounds to our right and we turned as one to see what made them. I've been scared before. But this was the first time I'd ever been so frightened that I knew what it was to be rooted to one spot.

Coming up at us with the speed of express trains were some ten or fifteen animals the likes of which I'd never seen. They were part lizard and part elk. There was the head of an elk mounted on a lizard's body. But such a lizard as I didn't believe existed. I didn't wait for Hank's shout of warning. I had already turned and started downward for the place we had just quitted. But my terror rose to a fevered pitch when I saw that there was nothing there. The room or vehicle of transport into this strange and terrible world had disappeared. There was nothing but the convulsed earth and boulders.

It wouldn't have made any difference anyway. These monstrous beasts were too swift.

Now there was the sound of voices about us, English voices; commands to halt, shouts of anger and some of speculation. Then above the others, a bull-like bellow:

"Stop, fools. Stop ere we rip you apart!"

We came to a sliding stop and side by side waited for, I guess, death. The beasts ground to dust-clouded stops. Then as their riders dismounted they looked at us through their soft strangely gentle eyes. But there was nothing peaceful or gentle in the eyes or faces of the men who surrounded us. Oh no…they looked fierce and very unwelcoming.

I essayed a grin and swallowed hastily as the first of them came close. Beside me Hank's breath whistled shrilly as he tensed in anticipation of battle. Not that we stood any chance if there was going to be. Not with the way these babies were adorned.

Insofar as size was concerned they looked no bigger than most men from where we'd come. Nor were they any different in facial or physical characteristics, except maybe in fierceness of looks. It was just their get-up. They wore little helmets, serrated and adorned with a strip of feather. Their chests were covered by a wide strip of metal leaving their bellies bare. They wore gauntlets of the same metal and their legs were also covered to some three inches above their knees. The metal was very flexible because it gave as they walked. From their waists to where the leg covering began was a kind of link-metal skirt. It rang metallically as they moved about. There was a belt of leather about their waists. From it hung, on one side a dagger, and on the other a sword.

"Who are you? From whence come you?" asked one who was evidently the leader. He was the biggest and certainly looked the most fierce with a scar that ran the length of one cheek to his chin, giving him a most terrifying look.

My mouth opened and closed, opened and closed but no sound came out. It was Hank who took the lead:

"I am Henry Sharpe. And this is Berkeley Livingston," he said. "We come from—from Chicago," he ended weakly.

I knew how he felt. But what the devil were we to say to those questions.

THE leader of this strange troop mulled the words over to himself as though they were some strange food he was tasting. His eyes were on the ground as he mumbled to himself. Suddenly they lifted and pierced us with their fiery glance. I felt my knees turn to water at that uncompromising stare. I knew I was too young to die.

"Of this place from whence you come I have no knowledge," the big guy said. "Perhaps Loko may have. He is all-wise. Mount these men and let us be off before we are discovered. We are still a long way from home."

Immediately his men began a tuneless whistling at which their strange mounts came trotting. One of them gave me a hand and I slid up until I sat just outside the pocket of the flat saddle they used. Hank too was lifted to the back of one of the elk-lizard deals and in an instant we were off. And I mean off and running! How those babies could travel! They'd have walked off with all honors at any track in the country.

I don't know exactly how long we rode. Time had no meaning. Our watches had stopped. The sun stood at the zenith all the time. All I know is that my back was sore, my legs were numb and that this character behind whom I was riding had never taken a bath in his life. The only thing that held meaning for me was the changes in scenery. For perhaps a mile after we started the road or path or whatever it was we followed was level and flat. Then we came to a forestland into which we rode with the same abandon as before. The trees were thick and the branches often swept low so that I was continually ducking to stop from being swept off my mount. This went on for hours, it seemed. Then we were in the open again. But the topography had changed. The gentle slopes were gone. This was hill country, rough and a little frightening. We didn't ride directly upward but at a long slant. I didn't notice at first but later I observed that we always rode where there was some sort of shelter. The open places were avoided with assiduous care.

My fears lessened or dulled, as the ride went on interminably, and I looked about with more appraising glances. For a land which held the appearances of care there were less people about than I would imagine there to be. Since the sun was always at zenith, time had little meaning, at least in the sense we have of time. This might be the time for sleep or dinner or lunch or breakfast for all I knew. At least they were reasons for the lack of activity in this weird place of ever-sunlight.

Suddenly I was hungry. But I mean hungry. It wasn't just a gnawing feeling. It was a biological flood of demands for food. My rider was in the center of the troop. Hank was up ahead somewhere not far from the leader. I was too far back to see the gesture, which was the command to halt, but there came shouted words from ahead:

"Halt! Eat. Eat…"

My rider kicked with his right heel at the leathery side of the beast we were riding and the monster slid to a halt. We slid off and joined the rest. I was stiff and sore as I found a seat beside Hank on a grassy hummock. There was a far-away look in his eyes and it wasn't one of hunger. For once my interest was not on his thoughts or mood. I was *hungry*.

I GUESS I looked my disgust when I saw the meal we were to have. It came from saddlebags, which were attached to the animals we had been riding. My riding companion strode up to me and held the unappetizing piece of leathery whatever-it-was in his hand.

"Well, bless your little…" I said. "That's decent of you, old man, I must say."

He had a half smile on his lips as he stood there with the stuff in his hand. At my words the smile went away, but fast, and his free hand shot out and cuffed me alongside the jaw.

"I am not an old man!" he said in vicious tones.

Now, I'm a peace-loving individual. The sort of guy, in fact, who will not just walk away from trouble, I'll *run* from it. Comes a tavern brawl and I'm the first to head for under the table. In an argument I'm the oil-spreader. So maybe it was that I was hungry and tired and sore. Or maybe I was guttier than I thought. But suddenly before I could reason I was on my feet and at this character.

I hit him with a left and right and another left and right, all on the puss. Then I shot one to his belly and he folded up like a wind-broken accordion. A last right, this one on the button, and he spun away for about ten feet to land flat on his back.

It all happened pretty fast. Faster than the telling of it. What happened after was just as quick. Instantly, the rest of these characters came at a run, the big guy who was bossman at their head. He looked down at the schmoe on the grass looking up at the blue, with vacant eyes, then looked at me. There was a puzzled glint to his eyes.

"What happened?" he asked.

I was surprised at the politeness of tone.

"I don't go for slapping around," I said.

"No? I must tell you then," he said in that same polite tone, "that certain formalities must be observed. As soon as Hago has recovered his senses he will ask for reprisals. It is the custom here, my friend."

"Yeah?" Hank said sharply, as only a Sharpe can ask. "And what will those be?"

"Edged with tips of steel of course," the big guy said casually.

"Hey…" Hank said angrily. "Berk doesn't know anything about dueling with swords."

Nor about dueling with anything else but my mouth, I thought. Maybe we could fight a duel that way. Of course I hadn't done badly with my fists…

The big guy shrugged his shoulders and all the metal he carried clanked an accompaniment. Hank brought up another point:

"Besides, Berk doesn't have the protection of armor."

"Then it will be over quickly," the big goon said.

Suddenly Hank grinned. A fine time to smile, I thought. I was going to die, and Ray Palmer wasn't going to get that story after all, and all Sharpe the sharpy can do is laugh about it. My bosom buddy. My pal. Hank, I thought, if ever you ask me to listen to one of those corny jokes you like to tell, I'll throw Joe Miller down your throat.

"And what of Loko?" Hank asked. "Won't he be angry?"

The big guy stroked the scar on his cheek. He nodded several times as though in agreement with what Hank had brought up. Then he too smiled and I thought; Hank, bosom buddy, you're a prince. With the wit you're fast like a rabbit. Now why didn't I think of that?

"Yes. Loko would be angry, especially if he knew there had been two of you and I brought only one in…"

BOTH Hank and I stopped smiling. The familiar chill found its groove and raced down my spine. I didn't need an interpretation of what he said. In effect, the less Loko knew the less he would be angry about.

The rest of the gang, with the exception of Hago, had gathered around while the palaver had been going on. They ringed us in with a fence of steel for their swords were out. I looked from face to face and found nothing in any to give me hope of the future. I swallowed the lump, which formed in my throat and wished I could be brave and come up with the kind of quip the usual storybook hero has in a moment like this. Blank. That was my mind.

But not Hank's. He had things to say. I wished he hadn't. Seemed like every time he opened his yap trouble came out.

"Is this how you welcome strangers?" he asked.

If nothing else the big guy liked to chew the fat!

"Strangers are never welcome here on Hosay. They are always troublesome. This way our troubles, and yours, incidentally, will soon be over, and the path of our lives will be smooth again."

"We didn't ask to come here," Hank said.

That was a lie, but at this point of the game I didn't think it made any difference.

"No? Then how did you come?"

"Luria made us," Hank said.

By all that was holy, I'd forgotten about the gorgeous doll who had brought us this trouble. I remembered now and blessed her with a few choice epithets, none of which would look nice in print.

"Luria!" his voice rose until it almost sounded feminine. "She brought you across the void? Ho-ho! Loko will surely want to see you. Well, Hago can wait his vengeance for a bit. I don't think you will be leaving Hosay very soon… Well, we've spent enough time in talk. Let us eat and be off again."

Funny how my appetite got lost. I took maybe two bites out of the leathery stuff. But even though I'd lost my hunger I had to admit to the tastiness of the stuff. Then we were back in the saddle and riding hell-bent for wherever they were going. Whether my muscles had grown used to the grueling pace or just that I'd grown numb I don't know. But now I didn't feel so weary. So that in the end when we topped a rise and came to the valley that held the tribe of Loko, I felt an odd sense of awareness of things.

I say it was a valley. Actually it wasn't. But on first appearance it seemed that. Rather to be proper it was a plain that stretched for a vast distance and lay between two ranges of hills that were not quite high enough to be called mountains. As we rode down the shallow pass, which led to the city, I speculated on the familiarity of the place. As we got closer I knew what the resemblance was. It looked like the stretch of pueblos in Taos, New Mexico. Of course there was the difference of soil conditions and mountain stretches. But I'm speaking of the habitations. Our coming had been noticed long before our arrival and a great number of riders came dashing out to meet us, all mounted on the elk-lizards.

They yelled, shouted, and waved their swords about as they closed in on our small company. Pandemonium is a long word, but it's the only one that fit the situation. We must have stretched out for a good mile as we rode down the long street between the pueblos until we reached the one that was the most imposing, the one that was a good five stories high.

This one was different from the rest in that instead of a ladder, it had a broad staircase, which circled about the entire structure. Then, while the others waited, Hank and I, between several guards, mounted the staircase and proceeded upward behind the big guy who was the leader of the troop.

AT THE fifth story we came to a broad gate. There were armed sentries standing guard before it. Through the open latticework of iron I could see other men standing watch. Whoever Loko was he liked protection. The big guy exchanged words with the guards, who in turn called something to those inside and the gates swung open. There was something ominous in the way those huge iron things closed behind us.

Once more we went on the march. We had come into a shallow courtyard. Birds of brilliant plumage sang from trees. The courtyard was circular with several entrances to the building we had as our goal. The center entrance was for us. Straight for it and into the coolness of a vast room where all was peaceful the big guy led us. Here we came to a halt. I looked about and wondered why we stopped here. The room had but a single entrance or exit, the doorway through which we'd come. The answer came in a few seconds.

Suddenly we started to rise, all of us. And I knew we were on a sort of platform much like that of a stage. It was then I saw the openings high in the walls above. There were three, quite large. When we reached the level of these openings the platform stopped its ascent, and once more we stepped forward. Again it was the center opening that was our goal. This too had guards and after the usual exchange of talk we were allowed entry.

It was a long rectangular room in which we found ourselves. At one end was a dais on which was a long table. There were six men sitting at this table. The walls of the room to either side of the dais held couches and seats. The room was empty but for the men up ahead. We were led forward until we stopped some fifteen feet from the dais. Then the big guy stepped forward.

"Mighty Loko," he began. "I am Captain Mita, in charge of the group who went in search of the holy Groana bird. I have come before your greatness with a strange story…"

All the while I'd been giving this Loko character the once-over. I didn't know he was Loko until Mita called him by name. But he *was* the sort of person you give a second and even a third glance. The trouble was I didn't look at the rest. Not until Hank nudged me and whispered from the side of his mouth:

"The women! Look at them."

It was small wonder that I hadn't noticed them. As I said, I thought there were six men up there in front of us. They were all dressed alike except Loko. Their uniforms were much like Mita's except they were more elaborate with jewels sending showers of varicolored lights at us. Then I saw the breastplates and realized for the first time that of the six people up there four were women.

The fifth was a giant of a man, easily, even though he was seated, better than seven feet tall. The sixth was Loko. He was dressed in a toga-like gown, which fell in a straight line from his thin wrinkled neck to his feet. From the center of the toga straight down the center was a line of color demarcation. One side of the robe was a bright purple, the other a deep green. Then Loko started to talk, and I forgot all else:

"Who are these two? From whence come they? And how did you come upon them?"

CHAPTER THREE

CAPTAIN MITA related how he found us. All went well until he mentioned Luria. I thought they'd leap down our collective throats so great was their excitement. All but Loko. His lean face didn't show a muscle change and his eyes peered narrowly down at us as though their piercing glance could read what lay beneath the flesh and bone of our foreheads. Their voices rose in shrill cacophony, the gist of which was we ought to be put to death immediately. Suddenly Loko raised a thin arm, which shook slightly.

"Peace! This chattering, as though you were but birds in the courtyard to whom had been cast seed. Peace, I say!

"Are your minds so dulled by the games of war that they see only what lies on the surface? Look ye well on these strangers. Do they have the look of any men we know? They have not spoken their minds yet but I'll warrant their speech is as foreign as their attire. They knew not of swordplay. One used his fists as a weapon. But all this non-observance can be forgiven. It is in the misconstruing of the fact they knew Luria that I speak. Let me assure ye they are accidental arrivals here on Pola. There are some things, which are as open pages to us. But the art of transposing humans from one plane of time to another is the closed page, which not one of us can open, for we have not the key. Not even Luria, the all-wise woman.

"Oman, the father of Luria, was the wisest man who ever lived. The small knowledge I have was gained at his knee. But even he, with all the secrets of the ancients at his mind's disposal could not do that. I do not say that she, in some fashion known only to her, was able to bring them across the great void between the land of the eternal mists, from the place from whence they came to Pola. But only these two came.

"I do not know who they are or why they were brought here, but look ye well on them. Can ye see the smallest sign in them which would bring harm to us or disturb the smallest detail of our plan?"

The old character was *right*. We were a couple of harmless schmoes. As far as I was concerned I had had my fill of this place. All I wanted was to be put back on that black cloud and taken back to that place, 'from whence we'd come.'

"However," he went on, "it would be of great interest to us to find *how, where and when* Luria managed all this. Shall we ask them?"

Mita's boys acted too fast for us to do anything about it. They were well trained. Loko had barely finished talking and our arms were pinioned behind our backs. I started to struggle but gave up as the guard's arms tightened about me. Yet a strange fact registered at the back of my mind, a fact I was going to put to use later, I knew. This guy holding my arms behind me was straining all his muscles in the effort and yet if I wanted to I could have quite easily broken his grip.

The guy who had been sitting beside Loko *was* better than seven feet tall. The instant we became helpless the five of them left their companion on the dais and swarmed about us.

"So they like to use the fist, eh?" he had a bellow like a bull. He stood spraddle-legged in front of us, his arms akimbo. He threw his head back and let out a roar of laughter. The sound echoed around the huge room. I had to strain to look up at him, he was that big.

"Sure," I said. "What's more, I'd use them on you too, you big schmoe…"

HE THREW a punch at me that was telegraphed like a slow freight through Missouri. I ducked just as it arrived. Only I forgot about the guy behind me. I ducked backward and my head cracked against his face and came forward in a rebound, smack into that ham-like fist. I won't say it felt like being hit by a pillow. On the other hand I've been hit a lot harder, a heck of a lot. I shook my head clear and grinned up at the no-longer smiling face.

"Better try again," I said. "That I can take all day."

Me and my big yap. Boy, did I take the lumps! He hit me with everything but the meat cleaver he carried at his side and he'd have probably used that except he was that mad. I was covered with blood, mine, and he was covered with glory, when he got through. At least it sounded like an ovation he got. I staggered to my feet and looked to where Hank was.

He had that beefy look around his jawbones too. It was the first time either of us had been jumped by a gang of women. I guess Hank was thankful this was one world where women didn't have the prerogative of scratching. He'd have been a lot bloodier than he was. On the other hand it isn't the most fun thing to have women pounding lumps on you.

But though his head was bloodied it wasn't bowed. He winked at me. I thought it *looked* like a wink. Of course with all that swelling around his eyes it could have been something else. I grinned back at him and the two of us turned to face the gang of mostly women that had jumped us. They were standing together just in front of the dais. Evidently they'd been talking to the old one at the table, Loko.

"I see," Loko said, "your planet breeds stubborn men. A pity. Because we have the means to undo those stubborn tongues. I would very much dislike causing any additional suffering. Unless, of course, you force my hand…"

"Perhaps," Hank managed to get out between his puffed lips, "if we knew exactly what you wanted, we might cooperate…"

Loko repeated the big question again. The others gave us searing looks and shoved their fists down to the hardware at their belts. But I was more interested in Hank. He had that thoughtful look on his face. It was kind of hard to figure what the look he had was due to the swelling. I just guessed.

"Okay!" Hank said in decisive tones. "It was like this…"

LOKO'S fingers sounded a tapping on the tabletop. He chewed his upper lip with his lower for a few seconds, then said:

"It has the ring of truth, this tale you tell. Enough to warrant a surety that in the tale is a greater part of it. I know that Oman, Luria's father, was interested in the transmigration of bodies from one sphere to another, though I didn't know he had gone so far. But the fact remains that it was an experiment, otherwise she would have met you two. Still, as things stand, perhaps she was busied in other matters…?"

One of the dames had cackled in laughter at the words. Her laugh was stilled at the look the old guy shot her. Yet it seemed to me that there wasn't anything in those mild old eyes to make *me* shut up that way.

"In any event, I think we had better place you in safe custody for the while. Captain Mita…"

"Sire?"

"Have these men placed in the cage on the topmost tier. And I shall expect a vigilant guard to be put over them. They are bait for the beautiful Luria."

I got it then. It was too late to do anything about it, of course. Because even as I turned to give battle, one of the boys behind me jabbed my spine with his steel tickler, and I turned yellow like a dandelion in the spring. I was going to be a live coward.

"Okay, wise guy," I said. "You win. As for you, you big schmoe," this to the lug who had taken his best shots on me, "some day you and I'll meet under better auspices and then…"

*　　*　　*

The gate clanged shut behind us. I stepped over to the pallet in the corner and sat on the straw. Hank stayed close to the bars, his back to me.

"Might as well take it easy, Hank," I said. "This looks like the kind of place that's going to grow on us. We might as well take it easy. Like I say, we might be here a long time."

"Y'know," Hank said, "something funny happened down there. When that guard grabbed me and held my arms behind me, I felt as though all I had to do was twist and he'd go flying."

I sat straighter. Hank too… I winced as I grinned in reply. The same thing had occurred to me, too. Maybe the big guy had damaged me a bit, but he hadn't knocked me cold.

"And knowing that that does us a lot of good here," I said sacastically.

"No, it doesn't. Nor did it do any good down there, either. Those stickers they had, carried more weight than our fists. It's just something we ought to keep in mind. Of course, the thing to remember now is that Luria knows we're here…"

"She does?" I guess my voice was a bit on the sarcastic side. He turned like a shot and stepped to my side. I didn't like the look in his eyes.

"Listen! And get this straight!" he snapped. "I don't want any wrong cracks about that girl…"

I laughed and waved my hands in a gesture of goodwill. "Just talking, Hank," I said.

His fingers waved a pattern in front of my eyes. "So stop talking and listen. She said she'd see us here. And not to worry."

"Not to worry, eh? Well, that's good to know. So what are we supposed to do while we're here, count the straws on the bed?"

"I don't know. She just said not to worry. That she'd get to us."

I GRUNTED something in disgust and stretched out on the straw. It got under my shirt collar, into my trousers, my ears and even in my socks. I thought, if she were going to get here, to do it soon. A little more of this and I'd go wacky. After a bit Hank got tired of supporting the bars and came down to sit by my side. He hummed a snatch of a popular tune. It was his way of being deep in thought. Me, I was also deep in thought…thought of a steak at Gus's.

I'm a bit deaf in one ear and after listening to that tuneless humming of Hank's for a while I turned my good ear to the straw and faced the wall. The masonry wasn't in too good of condition. In fact it was cracked and flakes of grey stuff lay like dandruff on the surface of the wall. I began to peel some of the stuff. It peeled like wallpaper, and like wallpaper, some of it stuck. I yanked at it, then in anger punched at it. My fist almost went through the wall.

I yelped in pain and Hank turned to see what had happened. One look and he was crawling to my side.

"Hey," he whispered in excitement. "What goes?"

"I don't know," I whispered in return. "But this stuff's about as strong as oatmeal mush. Have a crack at it but first put your hanky around your knuckles."

As I said before, Hank, though a small man, had the muscles and hands of a carpenter. When he slammed his wrapped fist into that masonry something gave and it wasn't his hand, which simply disappeared into the wall almost to his elbow. I knelt on the bed behind him, grabbed him about the middle and yanked backward. We fell off the bed as the hand came out of the wall faster than we thought.

"My gosh!" Hank said in disgust as he stared at the hole in the wall. "Are we dopes. There's a ram we could have used and we go around bustin' knuckles."

I knew exactly what he meant. The bed. It had a metal frame. In a few seconds the bed was apart. We used the long metal sides as rams. It wasn't more than a couple of seconds later that light streamed through the twin holes we made in the wall. What surprised me was that no one had heard us with all the racket we were making. But I certainly didn't care. Dust and bits of stone fell about us in a grey shower as we widened the holes into one large hole. It was big enough after a few moments for the both of us to crawl through side by side. So we did.

We came out on a sort of balcony. Since the building was circular the balcony was also circular. There was a ledge perhaps a couple of feet high acting as a break against the straight drop. I peered downward and saw that there was no escape that way. And we had to escape. Because the instant we were through, the patrons of this bastille began a caterwauling of sound that should have awakened the dead. Only it wasn't the dead we were worrying about.

"Up! The roof. It's our only chance," Hank shouted and started up the sill of the prison we'd just quitted.

The wall, I saw then, was not flat or smooth. There were serrations and rough spots, which were deep in the stone. One didn't have to be an acrobat to ascend but it would have helped. Then we were on the roof.

As far as I could see we hadn't gotten anywhere except up. But Hank had other thoughts. He started at a run for the far end away from the center. I followed. What else was there to do? I saw when we got there why he had headed for it. As I said in the beginning, the buildings were constructed like pueblos. We were looking down at a setback that was only a half-story below us. Hank, being an artist, had formed a picture of what the interior had to be like from what he saw of the exterior. It was a long jump but we didn't hesitate a second. I landed in a heap beside Hank.

Instantly we were up and heading for the next setback. We knew the alarm would not be long in sounding.

We made the second; three more to go, I thought, as we raced for the third. This time we didn't quite make it. There were many openings on this level. And as we started for the jump-off place, men began to pour from these openings. We ran like scared rabbits, but they had the speed of deer. There were some twenty or thirty waiting for us at the edge.

We slowed to a walk, then to a stop. As usual their stickers were facing our way.

"SO," LOKO said in wearied tones. "You are strong men. Prisons do not hold ye. Then we shall have to throw ye into a something that will. I did not want to do what I am going to unless my hand was forced. Ye have forced it. Throw them into the pit..."

There were a lot more guards this time. Our march to this pit Loko spoke of was almost a processional. The whole village turned out to see us—men, women, and children. I noticed that this tribe was a tribe of warriors. All, men, women, and children bore arms. They were neither gentle in appearance or in their manners. We received the physical manifestations of a Bronx cheer in the parade to the pit. I learned there were many strange and ill-smelling vegetables on Pola. Some of the kids threw them at us with a very good aim.

The guards thought it was good fun until several of them got hit in the head by some bad throws. Then they shagged the kids. By that time we'd reached the end of the pueblo city. The way led up and down hill for several miles. Toward the end of our journey there were just a few of the villagers left, all women. I got a very strong impression that the women were actually far more savage than the men. There was something so frightening in their bright looks, as if they would just as soon have our deaths over with on the spot.

We reached our goal at last. I know I breathed a sigh of relief. Whatever we had to face in the pit would not be as frightening as those women.

It was a strange pit, for it was located on a high, earthen tower that stuck upward like a lonely finger on the bosom of the plain. A long series of steps wound around the tower to the very top. We were forced to walk ahead, the prodding swords acting as an incentive. At the top we found another series of steps, these leading downward from a platform on the top. I hadn't time to observe much, but I did notice that the top of the earthen tower had been leveled flat so that a great many people could be accommodated on the surface.

As Hank and I wound our way down we noticed that circular openings had been cut into the face of the tower. Our way led evenly between these openings. I became aware of strange odors, bittersweet, an acrid stench that turned my stomach the more I got a whiff of them. We could see before we passed them that these openings had bars before them. Odd muffled sounds were heard. Once we were startled out of our wits by a roaring sound, which, if it did come from an animal, must have been the largest beast in any world. It made a lion's roar sound like a mouse's squeak.

Going up, we were close to the face and going down we were too busy in the descent. But once we reached the bottom and looked upward we saw how far we were from the top. The blasted thing looked miles away. There were fly specks on the platform way up there. We saw them busying themselves at something. And suddenly there was a vast clattering sound and the stair, down which we'd come, reversed itself. One problem was answered. If we were to escape, it would not be by way of that winding staircase.

"Shall we dance?" Hank asked.

"Yeah," I said, looking about me. "To the Dance Macabre."

CHAPTER FOUR

HE SAW what I meant. The floor of the huge circular pit was covered by innumerable stains. One glance was enough to tell us only blood left that particular stain. As if that wasn't enough, the whitened bones of hundreds of humans were scattered about. Many a party had been thrown by the lads and lassies of Loko's ménage.

"D'ja notice," Hank asked, "that although the sun hasn't stopped shining for a single second we haven't felt any discomfort?"

"What's more peculiar," I reminded him, "is that we have no desire for sleep. I'm speaking for me of course."

"Right. And I'm not hungry either."

"Let's hope the zoo isn't hungry," I said.

"Could be, Berk," he said after a moment's silence, "that we won't get out of this spot."

"Speaking of zoos," I said, "wonder how our friend Mokar and his mistress are making out?"

The funniest expression suddenly came into Hank's eyes, as though he'd been clipped by a phantom punch. He looked dazed. Words stumbled their way past his lips:

"Yes...I hear... We will...obey..."

I got scared and shook him. I certainly didn't need Hank to get screwy on me—things were bad enough. He came out of it a moment later. In fact he grinned quite like his normal self.

"What happened? Another séance with Luria?" I asked.

"Yes. Come on. We've got to get to the center of the arena. Loko wants us out of the way. His boys will be here soon."

Soon, it turned out, was that very moment. They must have been right on our heels. Suddenly the platform above was black with people. It was impossible to make out the figures of any.

"Yipe!" Hank howled. "Look!"

His quivering finger was pointing up toward the face of the earthen tower. A huge something was clinging to the sheer wall just below one of the openings. Slowly it began to crawl downward. There was something horrible in that sluggishly moving shape. It moved with infinite care yet with a surety that was startling for so large a thing. As it neared the pit we saw it more clearly. I've always wondered what it meant for blood to run cold. I knew then.

It was something from out of a nightmare. To a child versed in the fairy tales it was a dragon. To me, it was a prehistoric beast. It had a great triangular head and a massive body, which was scaled from the head to the long tail. Wisps of smoke trailed from its nostrils. I crowded close to Hank as though in mutual protection. And he in turn began a slow retreat to the point farthest from where the beast would land.

It must have stretched a good fifty feet!

The great mouth split and from the many-rowed teeth came a terrible stench. A roar split the silence of the pit as it shook its head from side to side. Then it saw us and began a cumbrous movement in our direction. We kept retreating until our backs were against the granite of the wall. It followed relentlessly…surely.

"You run one way," Hank breathed heavily. "I'll run the other."

Perhaps the beast had been used to easier prey. For as we split up and ran for the opposite wall, it stood still, its head moving from side to side as if in wonderment at our sudden disappearance. When it finally did move it was with express train speed, the murderous tail swishing about in a vicious swing.

ONCE more we faced it together, but this time from the opposite wall. We knew, however, that the respite we had gained was small. No matter how many times we ran from it, we had no place to go except in a circle. And sooner or later, we would have to stop from sheer exhaustion. Then...

Once more it lumbered toward us. And again we broke for the other wall. We were breathing a bit heavily as we faced the beast again. The faint echo of shrieking voices reached our ears and we involuntarily looked upward. We groaned in unison when we saw the reason for the shouting. They had let another of the horrors at us. We could see the huge body crawling down the granite wall.

"Run, *Berk!*" a voice screamed in my ear.

We had forgotten the beast. As we had looked upward it had moved forward, Hank spotting it first. He leaped to safety, but I wasn't that lucky. The very tip of the tail caught me as I tried to leap to one side and sent me sprawling. I said the beast had the speed of a train when it moved. I was barely on my feet when it was on me.

I had fallen close by a pile of bones. Stooping, I picked a thigh bone from the pile. And swinging it like a bat, I let the thing have it right across its ugly fire-spitting snout. Surely there was no hope or reason for my act. But I wasn't going to go down without at least one blow in my defense, no matter how puny it was.

I could only stare, open-mouthed, as the beast snorted loudly and retreated from me. With a wild yell spouting from my lips I followed it, belaboring it across the snout with my bone-bat. Hank, seeing what was taking place, came to my assistance. We were laughing, I guess in hysteria, at the way things were going. Then it happened—we had forgotten that damned tail.

One sudden swish and we were both knocked from our feet. And this time there were two of them at us. The second had arrived and was moving in. Their mouths seemed big enough to take us in at a single gulp. I had time for one prayer, as I tried to gain my feet.

I swear their teeth were only inches away when that terrific wind came up. My senses started to reel. I couldn't move a muscle, not even an eyelid. There was this wind, and this black cloud that came from nowhere. My ears rang with a shout... *"LURIA..."* And blackness enfolded me in a comforting blanket.

BERK! Berk!"

Wind was sweeping past me in a constant wave. It cooled my sweaty brow. There was a strange up-and-down movement. I opened my eyes and grabbed tightly at what lay beneath me.

"You okay, kid?" Hank asked.

He was directly ahead of me, in fact so close we were twins on Mokar's back. Hank's right arm was about Luria's waist. She had saved us from the very mouths of our doom. I didn't care how she did it nor was I interested. In fact I didn't have time to worry about the fact that we were riding on the back of a panther. I only knew I was alive. It was enough for me.

But after a few moments of this pounding run I began to sit up and take notice. For one thing, Mokar was running so smoothly, in such marvelous bounds, that the action was slick as oil. For another thing, the surroundings were exotic in the extreme.

We were in the midst of a jungle. The trees were magnificent in their height and variety. Birds of brilliant colored plumage sang from bush and branch. The air was invigorating and surprisingly free of humidity. Mokar was sure-footed. His lithe shape never disturbed a single branch as he moved along an invisible trail. Luria sat high up on his body close to the muscled shoulders. She was clothed in the same sort of costume I saw on the warrior women by Loko's side. A slender, needle-tipped spear was couched along one elbow. She looked straight ahead.

The jungle ended abruptly and we entered a grassy plain set in gently rolling hills. Mokar's pace never slackened though our weight must have been considerable even for him. The miles flew by in endless procession. Then with a suddenness that took my breath away, while we were in the midst of what looked like bundles of straw, hundreds of shapes came to life.

The bundles of what I thought had been straw, were humans. And not a single one of them was a man. I didn't hear Luria give voice to any command, yet Mokar slowed his pace and after a very short while stopped running altogether. Luria slid from his back and Hank and I followed, although more gingerly. In an instant we were surrounded by the hundreds of chattering women. They're the same all over, the instant you give them a chance to talk, they start full blast.

But Luria didn't give them an opportunity to talk too long. Her arm with the spear held high shot up and silence fell among the warrior-women. As they gathered close I looked them over. There were short ones, tall ones, slim ones, and fat ones, beauties and ugly ones, calm ones and those whose eyes looked fierce enough to frighten Boris Karloff. In other words, they looked no different than those on the planet we'd quitted what seemed like years before.

NOT all were giving Luria attention. There were some who stole glances at us. There was one in particular. She was rather tall, certainly taller than I, whose hair was the color of molten gold, whose eyes were sapphires swimming in a sea of pearl. Her bosom rose high and well-formed in the breastplate she wore. And as she saw my admiring glance her breath quickened and her face flushed. I made a mental note that if the time ever came for talk, I'd forget to.

Luria nodded for us to step to her side. Then, as the others faced us, Luria began to talk:

"These are the ones I promised to bring. The secret my father, the great Oman, taught me has been put to use. But as he warned, I could not bring other than their bodies. Moreover, I could not foresee the place of their arrival.

"So misfortune came to them. One of Loko's bands found them before I could reach them, and brought them before the tyrant. Warriors! Loko threw them into the *pit...*"

A gasp of horror went up at the words.

"Yes," Luria went on. "Into the pit. Strangers on the planet of Pola. Loko violated again the holiest words of my father. Oh, that he were alive..."

"Mighty Oman, may his soul leave the place of its abode and help us," the women intoned solemnly.

Hank and I kept stealing puzzled glances at each other. But our curiosity had to contain itself. We knew that a lot of answers would soon be given.

"...His thousand years of reign brought Pola a great peace after the tens of thousands of years of wars. Now Loko has it in mind to break that peace. He has even enlisted the aid of *men...*"

This time the women's voices rose in a vast shout of anger. And once more Luria went on:

"...Aye! Men like Hostal, and Mita and others of his ilk. That was why I went out of our time and place and into another. To bring back the sex which once ruled. Our men have grown soft to the ways of war. They have grown soft because the years have made them that way. Look at the weapons of our fighting. Swords, spears, and knives. But we are fortunate. Loko and his minions have no choice in this matter. We must prevent Loko and his from gaining the upper hand. Else we all become slaves to his will…"

It was all going in one ear and out the other. But not Hank. He got it right away. I saw the heat of anger come to his eyes and face, but not in time to stop him. Whirling swiftly, he pulled Luria about until she was facing him.

"So that's why you brought me here? As a guinea pig! As a symbol for these Lysystratas of yours…"

Luria didn't take his fingers from her wrist. Instead, she motioned for the other women to halt; at the very touch of Hank's fingers, swords flashed in the bright sunlight and bodies tensed.

"Did you think it was because of your manly beauty?" she asked. "Or because of your charm?"

Hank's fingers fell away from her wrist. The flush of anger still lighted his lean long face. But there was a tinge of frustration in his eyes. Perhaps he *had* assumed it *might* have been because of some such reasons.

"I brought you here, you and this ugly wart of a man whom you call friend, because you were the vessel in which the fluid of my father's wisdom coagulated. Only *you* heard the call. And because this Berk was your friend did I allow him with you…"

"Okay," Hank said evenly. "You called, we answered. Now I don't like the set-up. So suppose you send us right back to the place you got us from."

"You pout prettily," Luria said. "How like must this Earth be to our planet. Here, too, the men pout if we do not give them their way."

I DAMNED her and could have kicked Hank. He kept opening his yap and she kept putting her foot in it.

"Yes," I said. "We have all the manners of men. But I gather you are not too well acquainted with *all* the ways. Perhaps it's in the cards that you're going to learn."

"Aah! He gives a twist to words and has no fear that they will rebound to confound him," Luria said, turning her attention to me.

I didn't care. There wasn't a dame alive on this or any planet I couldn't argue with or against.

"Yep. I have no fear. Only in your tears do you have immunity…"

"*Tears!* Do you take me for a man?"

I gave her a slow up-and-down. This time it was she who burned bright red. I knew my look was an insult. I'd already figured out that the boy friends and husbands of these Amazons were weak-kneed neutrals.

"Not the way you stack up, kid," I finally answered.

I guess it was insult direct. Only the answer to it came from an unexpected corner. My head rocked from a blow and I staggered a bit before I recovered my balance. When my head cleared I saw it was from a luscious girl whom I'd been admiring a few moments before. She now stood facing me.

"It is not meant that our leader, whose toes you are too low to touch, should deal you the punishment you deserve. But I, who am the smallest of her servants, can and will…"

I looked at Luria who had a half-grin on her lips.

"Teach the little toad a lesson," Luria said.

"Hey!" I called in protest as an immense circle formed about us. "I can't hit a woman."

And once more my head rocked as she planted one right on the jawbone. Well, woman or no, she wasn't playing for fun. I stepped back, danced around a bit to loosen up my leg muscles, put up my dukes and, *whammm!* Something hit me with the force of a mule's kick.

"Berk," a voice called from a long distance off. "Get up. Don't let her look like a champ…"

There were ten suns up there, and a million women at least. Then my head cleared and there was that beautiful pan looking down at me. I motioned for her to step back and got to my feet.

"Okay, kiddo," I said, snuffling the claret back up my nostrils. "You asked for it. Come and get it."

Then bing, bing, bing, faster than the telling takes, she let me have it.

My head was spinning and I thought I was hearing sweet singing birds all around me. I was seeing the faces of angels, too—just like in heaven. And once more Hank's voice called to me. I was beginning to dislike Mister Sharpe. Why didn't he take a couple of lumps?

The birds I thought I heard were the strident sounds of all the women yelling, and the angels' faces turned out to be not so angelic, once my vision cleared. My knees were on the wobbly side. My female adversary could hit like Joe Louis. I assayed a grin but yipped in pain instead.

"Enough?" the dear girl asked.

I SHOOK my head. I'm a stubborn dope in some ways. But the memory of the giant who'd taken his picks on me had come to mind and suddenly I wanted to haul off at something.

I motioned her forward with beckoning fingers. This time I got there *first*. Instead of hitting with my right, I closed the beckoning fingers of my left hand and jabbed her right on the point of her stubborn chin. Her head went back and my right came over, but with all I had on it. There was a sharp *crack!*

And she went sailing through the air to land on a pillow of grass some fifteen feet from where we were battling.

They proved they were the opposite sex, then. Their voices rose like banshees on the prowl and with a single concerted howl they made for me. Nor were they joking. They had those three-foot long stickers out and aimed right for Hank and myself. Again Luria stopped them:

"Halt! Are we men that we attack like animals? Besides, Lovah has not signified defeat."

I cursed the day I'd ever seen this woman, the day I'd ever met Henry Sharpe, and most of all the day I went to the zoo with him. Now I *was* on a spot. This Lovah could just be that stubborn as not to give up easily.

Several of the gals had gone to Lovah's assistance. The kid was on the wobbly side as they brought her forward. My punch had raised a lump on the side of her jaw. And her eyes didn't quite have that superior look as she tried to look into mine.

"Better take it easy, kid," I said, picking my words carefully. "There's no sense in beating each other silly. You're far too pretty to get messed up…"

I guess it was the first time anyone had called her pretty. Though why not was a mystery to me. She could make my breakfast any morning of the week.

Her left hand came up and caressed the swelling and her eyes became a lot more natural, and something of speculation showed in their deep blueness. I held my breath, waiting for her answer. I blew it out in a deep sigh when she said:

"Enough…for the while."

Only Luria was smart enough to get the game I'd played.

"You *are* clever with words," she said, and this time there was no scorn in her voice. "Well, call your mounts. Enough time has been wasted…"

It was a command that was instantly obeyed. A tuneless whistling went up and like black demons called from their pits, hundreds of black panthers, much like Mokar in appearance, though none so large, rose, as though from the very ground. They loped forward and the women mounted them. Lovah gestured for me to step to her side. I did and she motioned for me to mount behind her. Then at a signal from Luria, who had again taken Hank behind her, we were off.

"Say, beautiful," I said as we started, "you've got a wallop. And you've got a whole lot more that appeals to me, too."

She turned and looked deeply into my eyes. Her face became oddly soft. Then with the speed of light it changed, and as she drove her elbow into my belly, knocking the wind from me, she said:

"You've got a wallop, too…"

CHAPTER FIVE

AT FIRST I thought it was suburbia. At least a real-estate agent's dream development. They called it Gayno, but it could have been the community of El Rancho Grande, for all of me. It was a community of well-laid-out homes, all single-storied, with the most modern architectural designs; sloping roofs, glass walls, patios and terraces to take advantage of shade and sun gave it the House Beautiful look.

When we were still several hundred yards from the village of homes the women lifted their voices in a sort of musical chant. It was the first I knew their voices could be soft and charmingly feminine. Then, as we swept into the level grass-filled width of street, a host of men and children came from the houses and followed us to one set apart from the rest. Luria, in the lead, drew Mokar up to the shallow series of steps leading to the door of the house, and dismounted. Lovah kicked her panther beside Mokar and with a well-placed blow of her elbow, knocked me from the animal. As she wheeled him around, she turned her face to me and winked broadly.

I sighed deeply and got to my feet and walked to the side of Hank and the girl. I had an idea that this Lovah lady wasn't too displeased with me.

"Well, come in," Luria said.

The other women scattered as we followed the girl into the house. If I thought the exteriors of the homes looked like something out of House Beautiful, the interiors took my breath away. Two-level interiors with an incline leading to a combination dining and living room on the second story.

The first floor had four walls of colored glass which softened the sun's rays and gave them a subdued and marvelous brilliance, which somehow did not hurt the eyes. There was a wondrous air of peace and serenity in this house.

Luria slumped wearily into a deep-piled chair after throwing off her belt and helmet. There were a couple of sofas facing each other across a gigantic coffee table. Hank and I sat side by side on one, so that we were in profile to the girl. To our left was a raised fireplace of colored stones. Above it, on the mantle, were some statuary, primitives, from the looks of them. At sight of them, Hank arose and examined them closely.

"Say...these are truly wonderful. Who was the carver?"

"One of my servants," Luria said in answer. But her mind was elsewhere. She shook her head after a second or so, looked up to Hank and said, "Care for a beverage?"

"Sure," I said. "Make mine Scotch and water."

Hank was still deep in study of the small statue. He turned and said:

"Servant? Why that's almost criminal. Someone with a positive talent for creative work, someone with the ability of this person, whoever he may be, should certainly not be a *servant.*"

"Sit down," Luria said. It wasn't said in anger but rather in an almost supplicating tone.

HANK sat deep in a corner of the wide sofa. To my surprise she walked around the arm of the sofa, past the coffee table and faced us. She studied us for a second, then spoke:

"You are strangers here, in a strange land, among strange people who have strange customs. I don't have any doubts but that you will both have to spend the rest of your natural lives here. My father discovered the secret of transmigration of bodies. But it is still a mystery to me how he returned them.

"Therefore I beg of both of you to take what I have to say to heart. There should be a beginning, I know. But that beginning goes back into an antiquity greater and more distant than any you know. I saw a something in your eyes the instant you entered my home. I think I interpreted it correctly. You both marveled that you should find something approximating your own civilized world, after a visit to the world of Loko.

"Then let me start from there. For it is in that you might best understand. Here, you have a ready comparison. This land of Gayno and Loko's world. Further, when my father lived, there were better worlds, finer cities, greater cultures. But death came to him as it must come to all and though he lived to be eleven hundred and sixty-four years…"

I couldn't help it. Eleven hundred and sixty-four years! I grunted an unintelligible something. She caught on fast.

"Unbelievable, isn't it? That one can live so many years?" she asked.

Hank got the connotation of her remark before I did. He squinted at her and said:

"And I suppose you're in your…?"

"I am nine hundred and twenty-four years old," she said.

"Pretty well-preserved for your age, I'd say," I said.

"Lovah is almost a thousand years old," she said.

"Let's get back to your father," Hank suggested.

"Very well," she replied. "In the last forty years of my father's reign, a small border clash became a conflagration which set all of Pola aflame. He did not know it at the time, but there were some who were envious of his power. They plotted his downfall and overcame his legions. It turned into a war of utter annihilation. When it was over, there was nothing left of culture, civilization, or people. Here and there were scattered the fragments of humanity.

"They went back to living as they had done thousands of years ago. They had to do this because my father in his great wisdom, realizing the finality of the battle, doomed the terror weapons of the time and erased their marks forever. We, the offspring of that terrible time, had only the means you see of waging war, a sword, a spear, and a knife.

"So we had to make the best of things. For my people I chose the standard of living that best suited our time. I utilized the forms of home architecture that, because of the constant sunlight, would be most suitable. But, as I said before, we were scattered over the entire face of Pola. Loko, who was the ringleader and the only one of the Inner Council to survive the war, went back even further in antiquity for the plans of his community. But he wasn't interested in how his people lived. He still had it in mind and to this day is obsessed, by his overweening desire to be the ruler of the planet of Pola..."

WHEN SHE paused for a breath, Hank broke in. "Aside from the physical manifestations of what transpired with Berk and myself," Hank spoke up like a good scientist, "there are certain questions that are bothering me. I would appreciate it very much if an answer were forthcoming.

"Now then, I believe I am assuming correctly, when I say that Pola and the planet from which we have come are existing in the same spheres of time and space...?"

Good old Sharpe, I thought. Now he's going to make like he knows what he's talking about. Of course Hank always had a sharp mind, if I'm allowed a pun. He was proving it now.

Luria answered, "That is right."

"Well," Hank said in a speculative tone, "that proved a theory that some men have always held. Now another question. How is it you speak, in fact all the people we have met speak, our tongue, English?"

Luria smiled, arose, and walked to a near wall. A heavy ribbon-like cord hung against the wall. She puled at it and from somewhere in the house a bell sounded in answer to the bell-pull. She came back to the sofa and snuggled up in a corner.

"The tongue we speak is universal on Pola," she said. The instant you landed you too, spoke our tongue."

It wasn't a satisfactory answer but I supposed it had to do. Hank wasn't through, however.

"That doesn't make sense. Try this; what is the Groana bird and why is it holy?"

We had to wait for the answer to that. A husky, masculine voice said:

"Greatness... You rang?"

We turned and there was a man who was wearing a sort of lavalava for a costume. His hairy chest was bare as were his legs. Muscles rippled along the shoulders and arms and as he bent his legs knotted with muscles. He was close to six feet in height.

"Yes, Hioa," Luria said. "My guests are thirsty..."

He shook his head and as silently as he had come, he left.

"Are all your men servants?" Hank asked.

She nodded. "If not so in fact, in theory," she replied.

"A nation of women," I said. "All wrong."

"By Earthly standards perhaps," she said turning to me. "But as I said in the beginning, you must understand our customs *are* not as yours. Here, the women are the rulers. Men have only a minor part in the business of state."

I was tempted to ask something but I didn't think it to be the proper time.

"…Only Loko has changed those conditions of servitude," Luria went on. "Since the dawn of the new era, women took over the duties that men served so dishonorably before. All went well until Loko thought the time ripe. Secretly, he trained his minions in the arts of war, and when he thought the time was ripe, his campaign was started. He has a clever tongue. Not only did he manage to train the men of his tribe but he also convinced the warrior women of the Federation it was only for the purpose of waging war upon me that he did so—and that as soon as he had defeated me, he would relegate them to their former positions."

"And the Groana Bird?" Hank asked again.

"The Groana Bird is the symbol by which we will conquer," Luria said. "It is the most ancient of all living beings on Pola. It holds the secret of all things. It means success or failure. Once it sat on my father's right hand. Now it roams free and unfettered in the forest. We all seek it. And find it I must, even if I have to go into the valley of the mists…"

MY EARS pricked up at the sound of a screaming voice. I thought I was mistaken, but the voice sounded masculine. The screaming came closer. Then another voice joined it, this one raised in anger, and this one decidedly feminine. Hank and the girl heard the sounds also. An expression of displeasure crossed her face. She rose and started down the ramp. Hank and I followed.

We arrived at the front door simultaneously, Luria, Hank, I and the two who were screaming. Luria flung the door wide and a giant of a man sprawled to his knees before her. Behind him, some few feet came a short scrawny woman who held in one hand a thick club.

"Ohh, Greatness…" the character on his knees babbled. "Save me from Haavah. Save me…"

The women skidded to halt before us. The sounds of the screaming had brought others to their doors. I could see children huddled close to their father's knees. From the houses closest to ours, several women strolled over in curiosity. But at sight of the man on his knees before us and the scrawny woman who was standing with the club hanging limply from one hand, smiles broke on their lips. It was evident this story was not new to them.

"*Now* what is it, Jimno?" Luria asked in disgust.

"Haavah," the man babbled, "she beats me... I swear I have done nothing to deserve the beatings..."

"He lies, the idiot," the woman said. "through his teeth. Ten years we have been together. A simple thing like soup, and he burns it. It has become unbearable. I awake and it takes him a lifetime to make breakfast. Our children are the worst-dressed in the whole village. All he wants to do is sing..."

"Now ain't that too bad?" I said before Luria could say anything. "All he wants to do is sing, eh? Well, maybe we shouldn't waste sympathy on him. After all, he's so big and you're so small. I'm sure if he ever decided to give you your lumps, you'd be in bed for a week. Of course, he might have a bit of peace..."

"Quiet," Luria spat at me in anger. "I give the orders and dispense the justice in these cases."

"Sure," Hank said. "Close your trap. If we ever tell these characters that they're living in a fool's paradise they'll tear these women limb from limb..."

Haavah's face turned livid in anger. She turned on Hank and slapped him across the cheek. He went pale in anger and I saw his hands clench into bony fists. For the barest second I thought he was going to haul off and slug her. How he held back from doing it I don't know. I'm sure I couldn't have. Instead, he turned on his heels and went back into the house.

It was a mistake. Because I observed that the guy on his knees had been watching. There was a bright light in his eyes when Hank talked up like he did. But when Hank did the disappearing act, the light died.

The anger in Luria's face went into her voice:

"Haavah! We are becoming weary of this constant strife between you and Jimno. If it is true what you say and that you are as tired of it as you say, then haul him up before the bar of justice and have them sentence Jimno to the breaking of paavans to the halter..."

A CHANGE came over the woman's face at Luria's words. It reflected fear and horror now.

"Great Luria," the woman bleated. "Not that."

"And why not?" Luria asked. "He is of little use to you. Further he causes nothing but trouble. He sings when he should be doing the housework, he burns the soup, lets the children run ragged and uncared for, is lazy and a dozen other things. You will be better rid of him..."

"And he of her," I put in.

"But...the paavans. They have killed many who have tried to break them to the halter..."

"So he'll have a chance to prove he's either man or mouse," I said. "Certainly he's big enough as a man. Hmmm. If I had you for a wife, I'd know who'd do the housework and care for the kids. We teach women differently on Earth..."

"How is it done on Earth?" the man asked suddenly. He was still on his knees but his body was erect. And he was looking straight at me. So stunned were the two women by Jimno's temerity in speaking to me without asking their permission, they could only stare.

"She'd fit just right over your knee," I said quickly. "A couple of smacks with one of those palms and she'd behave, believe me…"

"Quiet, you!" Luria stormed.

But Haavah wielded a more efficient means of silence. She raised her club and clouted Jimno across the back of the head. A ripple of laughter ran across the narrow circle that had formed about the woman and her husband, as the man folded up in middle and sank face downward to the ground.

"Take him away," Luria said. To the paavans' compound. Let him break six of the beasts to the halter."

Suddenly I felt sick. Me and my big mouth. What had I done? Maybe I had sentenced a man to death? Anger whipped my voice to a frenzied shout:

"So this is the stuff from which you want us to weld a fighting force? And how do you expect us to do it, by the women whipping their men to us?"

From the corner of my eye I saw the man stir, shake his head and slowly get to his feet. Only I got the air of ominous quiet with which he moved. The rest watched him arise and an air of watchful waiting settled among the women. Dimly I felt someone standing by the door behind us. At the same time I realized that other doorways hid other watchers.

The woman, called Haavah, waited only until Jimno stood erect. Then with a movement that was altogether at variance with her scrawny self, she leaped forward and swung the club at the same time.

If I had ever been slugged like that I know I'd never have been able to duck that club. But he did. Then like a boxer who'd been hit hard and wanted to weather the storm, he ducked and weaved under and past the swinging club. The women thought the whole exchange was the funniest thing they'd ever seen. They laughed as the poor guy ducked, and once or twice they literally screamed hysterically as the club barely missed the curly black hair.

When he did move it was with unexpected speed. One second he was under the club, the next his fingers had wrapped themselves around it. With one twist it was pulled from her. He chuckled deep in his throat as he tossed it to one side. He motioned her forward. She didn't come so he stepped toward her. I yelled a warning as her hand sped to her belt. But he was speed personified as his hand beat hers to it. He twisted with an effortless movement of his wrist and her hand fell from the belt.

It was his free hand that went toward the belt now. I saw a dozen hands go for weapons as his fingers went about the circle of leather. He yanked downward and the leather parted. This too he tossed to one side. All the while his right hand held her wrist prisoner.

"Ten years, Haavah," his voice lifted in a singing shout. "Ten years…"

BUT Her face showed not the smallest sign of fear as he whirled her so that her back was to him. Then he had lifted her from her feet and dropping to one knee he laid her across that knee. She squirmed like a fish but without avail. His hand lifted and fell, palm downward. It lifted and fell. At first there was no sound but the whacking of her buttocks and the heavy breathing of the two. But after the tenth whack on the woman's shapely posterior, a whimper fled her lips. The whimper soon became a low moan, which soon became a distinct sobbing sound. It was strange, but not a woman stirred or spoke while he was administering the spanking. Nor did any lift a voice when he was done and said:

"Go, woman, and prepare me food."

Jimno stood tall and proud and faced his queen.

"The sentence still stands, Jimno," she said. "Haavah will cook and keep *your* house afterward. Beating her proves nothing."

"It proves he's a man," I said.

"Not by your standards. My women and I too, have broken the paavans to the halter. We've done this on many occasions. Let him go and try to do it. Then we can talk of manhood…"

"What is a paavan?" I asked.

"Mokar is a paavan…"

I turned and without a word went back into the house. I saw a shape slide into a passageway. I only got a glimpse of the figure. It was that of a man. His name was Hioa. Hank was deep in the sofa, cuddled up against one arm. He didn't hear me come in, his thoughts were so deep. I slid into the opposite chair and waited for him to come out of his brown study.

His eyes were bleak and bitter when he finally did turn. "Nice going, Sharpe," he said aloud. But he wasn't talking to me. He was talking to himself. "Now you can join the rest of the eunuchs…"

"Ah, cut it out," I said in disgust. "What the heck makes you that way. The gal's nuts about you."

"Sure. Just like that scrawny dame was about her man. Luria's probably been figuring in what womanly capacity I'd do best. Well, if she thinks I'm going to cook or scrub floors…"

I knew there was *one* way of breaking Hank from his thoughts. He wasn't the kind of guy who looked good playing crybaby. For one thing he was too big a man and I don't mean in size. But we had undergone a very strange and mystifying ordeal. Not that I'm such a big Joe about something like that. It's just that I'm thicker-skinned. Besides, I had some long range plans, most of which had to do with a Lovah gal… So I gave him the business about my troubles:

"You got worries," I broke in. "Your worries I should have…"

"What do you mean?"

"I just sentenced a guy maybe to his death."

"Huh?"

"Sure. I opened my mouth and that screwy dame, Luria, sentenced the poor Joe to break Mokar's buddies to the halter."

"She would," Hank said sourly.

"Yeah. And after he gave that silly fraulein of his a good tanning," I said.

"You mean the guy stood up for his rights?"

"That he did."

"Hmmm. Then maybe all hope isn't lost. Where's Luria?"

"Don't ask me. I had to walk away from it all."

"What do *you* want?" her voice asked from the direction of the ramp.

"To know one thing only, my pet," Hank said. "What is it you want of us exactly?"

"Just one thing. Teach my menfolk how to battle."

"Okay. But first teach your menfolk how to be men," Hank said.

And that was that for the evening or morning or whatever time it was in that land of eternal sun…

CHAPTER SIX

THERE were twin beds in the sleeping rooms Luria had given us. Hank and I slept in our undies. When we awoke we awoke to find the rest of our garments gone. In their places were breastplates and helmets such as Captain Mita and the other men in Loko's world, wore. We even had the long and short stickers to go in the belt that came with the metal apron that went over the short pants.

"She doesn't miss a trick," Hank said wearily as he stepped into the modern bathroom adjoining our bedroom. I heard the splashing sound of water but I was too engrossed in putting on the uniform that had been provided for me. Nor was it a bad fit. The only thing large was the breastplate. Of course I realized after a try-on that they weren't meant for a man.

The bathroom had everything but razors. My beard, which is of a dark texture anyway, hadn't known a blade's touch for several days, in fact from the looks of it, for a week. I remembered then that the few men I'd seen were either smooth-shaven or were hairless on the face. Hank gave a last sputter and stepped up from the sunken shower. He was rubbing himself with a fuzzy towel.

"Ain't no razor blades around here. I looked," Hank said. "Guess no one shaves out here." Then he looked at my new apparel. "How do they fit?"

I grinned at him. "They fit pretty well."

"Oh, well. Go on, take your shower. I'll see you later."

He wasn't in the room when I came back. Neither was his war garb. I donned mine and stepped out into the passage leading to the ramp. Here the bedrooms were on the lower floor. The two of them were already eating when I arrived. Hank gave me an okay sign with his thumb and index fingers, but the girl didn't even look up. We ate in silence.

"Well," she said after a last drink of something that looked like coffee but tasted like something else only better, "now that we're awake, suppose we get started?"

"You bet," I said, "and what does your *greatness* want us to do?"

"...When we get there," she said over her shoulder as she started for the door.

I gulped audibly when I saw what was awaiting us. Mokar and two of his brothers. Luria mounted her beast and looked to us. Hank and I glanced nervously at each other for a couple of seconds, then with ill-concealed reluctance, stepped to the sides of our mounts. The animals must have sensed our fear. As I started to lift my leg he turned his head and bared his fangs.

The fangs were very pretty in a savage way. I wondered who his dentist was as I backed quickly away from the spot I was in. Hank, on the other hand, had a lot more guts than I did. When his mount tried to pull a similar stunt, Hank cracked him over the nose. The beast's head came up and sideways. Hank slapped him again and jerked at the halter. Instantly the panther obeyed. Then Hank slid in the saddle.

And that left me on the ground.

"Oh, come now, nimble-tongue," Luria needled me. "We can't spend all day here."

"We can't?" I parried beautifully.

She looked past me and I turned to follow her glance. Directly behind us were a dozen of the biggest women I've ever seen. Not a single one was under six feet in height. And all were armed. As though in answer to a signal, one of them jabbed at me with one of those ten-foot-long spears they carried. It barely touched me, but the tip had a needle for a point. I yipped in pain and alarm. Then with a single leap I was in the shallow saddle. Teeth or no teeth, the spear was sharper.

We hadn't far to go. And after a while I got to rather like the ride. The panthers ran like the wind and the movement didn't have the up-and-down feeling of a horseback ride. Our destination was a valley. The valley was natural but it had been fenced in by a staked fence. As we approached one end of the valley, I saw that there was a gate. One of the warrior women dismounted and opened it. We rode in and found ourselves on a wide ledge overlooking the sheer drop to the almost circular valley below.

I LOOKED about and saw that a long series of steps had been cut into the stone. Below us something was taking place that caught and held my attention. At the far end of the valley I made out the shapes of four panthers. Coming toward them were a dozen women. These women were armed with spears. Behind them, unarmed, walked Jimno. We could hear the women crying to the panthers, telling them to take it easy. The animals suddenly broke and raced around the valley floor. Not all of them I saw after a second. One of them had been cornered. And for the first time I saw what Jimno carried in his arms, a bridle and halter.

I gasped when I realized what he was going to do, place them about the panther's throat. I watched his approach breathlessly. The only thing the women did was to hold the panther at bay with their spears. Jimno had to do the dirty work. And it was more than just dirty. It was dangerous. The beast snarled and showed its teeth. But I'll say this for Jimno. He walked in like it was a big tabby cat he was going to pet.

Suddenly there was a swirl of motion. A small cloud of dust arose. When it cleared we saw that Jimno had succeeded in placing the halter where it belonged. But his task was half-done. Now he had to ride the panther. Like a centaur, Jimno leaped onto the animal's back, kicked him in the ribs and began to work the reins. The animal snarled, turned his head to get at the man's feet but was only rewarded by slaps across its nostrils and kicks in the ribs. I was reminded of a cowboy breaking in a bronc. And to carry the similarity further, Jimno rode the panther back and forth across the floor of the valley until the panther obeyed the slightest touch of the reins or his feet.

The second and third beasts broke in as easily as the first. The fourth was another story. It was easily the largest of the four animals, even larger, I think than Mokar. It slapped the spears, once knocking down a woman who held one of them. If the others hadn't rushed to her defense he would have torn her limb from limb.

"Jimno had better be careful with this one," Luria said. "He shows a wild spirit."

Jimno must have realized it, too. His steps were far more careful. He walked daintily as though on eggs. The circle of spears opened to let him through. Sensing the helplessness of the man, the beast whirled to face him. Someone nearby was breathing in harsh, throaty gasps. It was me…

Down below the drama was becoming more tense. Jimno moved forward slowly, carefully. The beast retreated until at last its back was against the wall. Then Jimno did something strange. He paused when only a few feet from the panther, shook his head and dropped the gear he was carrying. He paused there erect and unafraid, then stepped forward. Instantly, as though the beast had been awaiting Jimno's action, it reared upward its front legs with those terrible claws open. And Jimno walked straight forward into the embrace.

I tried to yell, tried to get something past the sandpaper that suddenly lined my throat, but nothing came out. Even in the midst of terror, in circumstances which seem to hold one's entire attention, there is part of one that is separate from the rest. So it was I somehow saw Hank's and the girl's reaction to what was going on below.

Hank's face was rigid, livid with the tense expectation of what was sure to happen to Jimno, and horror-stricken that he couldn't help. Luria too showed emotion. Hers was rather like a surgeon in an operating amphitheater, watching a fellow surgeon at work.

Below, Jimno walked into the panther's embrace. But not to his death, as we were imagining. I don't know how he did it, but suddenly Jimno ducked. He must have ducked a split second before the beast slashed at him. But Jimno ducked the blow. And like lightning Jimno used both hands to grasp the panther by the fur at the shoulder. Then setting his feet hard in the earth Jimno swung the panther about and leaped on its back.

I COULDN'T help letting out a wild yell of delight. Nor was Hank far behind me with his cheer. Even Luria's eyes shone in admiration. For Jimno now had the panther at a disadvantage. He was on the beast's back, his fingers deep in the fur, his legs wound around the beast's belly. Jimno's right hand came up and delivered a terrific slap across the panther's face. The beast reared his fore claws and legs trying to swipe in futile swings at the man on its back. The more the beast clawed the harder Jimno slapped. At last Jimno was victorious. With a last vicious blow, Jimno slid from the panther's back and walked nonchalantly to where the women were standing.

He walked with his shoulders square and his back straight and when he came into their midst he didn't walk around them but moved as though they had better give him room, else he'd walk right over them. They moved out of his way all right.

He marched up the long flight of stairs, saw us, and came forward to stand before Luria.

"Greatness," he said, "the deed to which I was sentenced has been done…"

"And well-done," Luria said graciously. "Truly, you are a man, one worthy of carrying arms. Jimno, tell me. Would you care to be the first of the legions of men I am going to recruit?"

"I would be honored."

"Good. In the future you and Haavah will share equally the burdens and joys of your lives. If she lays a hand to you, you have my express authority to strike back…"

I realized I was hearing history being made. These men, though not eunuchs, performed the same functions.

"…So be it with you Jimno, and all men. Hear me, my lieutenants. From this day henceforth, all men share and share alike, the burdens and joys of women. On our return spread the news to the entire community. Go… You, Hank and Berk, stay with me. I have things to tell…"

She waited until the others had left, then dismounted from Mokar and walked to the lip of the valley and sat on a grassy hummock. Hank and I followed and sat beside her.

"…I was awake all night," she said. "Sleep would not come to me. My mind kept turning over and over again on the dilemma we are in. It is not an easy thing to admit defeat before it comes. Yet defeat is undeniable."

"Why?" Hank asked.

She tossed her head and her hair shook free in gleaming waves about her face.

"We are too few. Loko has not alone the majority of the tribes, but the very ones who have kept up a semblance of the war-like proclivities of their predecessors. We are their superiors in spirit, but in war, spirit alone is not enough."

"So?" Hank was doing one of those single-syllable deals with her. I knew it was irritating her because it was irritating me. Of course *I* knew the reason for it. She didn't.

"I have tried to find a way out of this situation, but the only one I can think of is to actually go to Loko and acknowledge his claim and throw myself on his mercy."

"If that's the way you feel..." Hank said.

I hid my grin with the palm of my hand. She was getting a little flushed in her cheeks. Spots of color burned below her eyes, eyes that were beginning to flash in anger. Her right hand, lying on the grass close to me, clenched in a small and capable fist.

"Okay then," Hank said. "Since that *is* the way you feel then send us back."

Her hand came down in a slap at the earth. Her lips set firm and hard against each other.

"Very well," she said. "I won't hold you here against your wishes. As soon as we get back..."

CHAPTER SEVEN

WE SAW the smudge of smoke lying low on the horizon when we were barely past the first hill. Luria's eyes widened at the odd sight, then narrowed in sudden understanding. I guess I was the last to catch on and so was the last to urge my beast to greater speed. I don't think we were very far from Gayno when we saw a horde of humans and animals coming toward us. In the lead, mounted on a magnificent panther, was Jimno.

We drew rein and waited for the arrival of the first of the mob. Jimno leaped from the back of his mount, dashed over to us and stood silent, his great chest heaving in panting breaths. We saw then that he had suffered a number of wounds, one of them a wide slash from a sharp instrument that had cut through the surface flesh all the way across the chest. Blood dripped from the wound, but Jimno seemed completely unaware of it.

"...Loko," he gasped after a second. He turned as the first of the hundreds of men, women and children streamed up, then brought his attention back to us. "Loko's minions attacked. While we were in the valley of the paavans. It was a surprise. And before a defense could be organized, they had set fire to the whole of the city. They were too many and the surprise was too great. Many perished. These are all who were left. I organized the retreat..."

They were a pitiful few, I saw, that had made good their escape. My eyes gladdened when I saw that the girl, Lovah, was among them.

"Then they will surely follow," said Luria, "perhaps they are not too far off. To the caves. Jimno, Lovah, and Berk, take twenty warriors and cover the rear. I'll take the others…"

"So get moving, stupe," Hank yelled.

I held both hands out emptily to show why I wasn't going anywhere. Immediately someone thrust a sword into one hand and a spear into the other, and to make matters completely at a loss for me, Hank kicked my mount in the rump and Lovah, Jimno, and I were off to glory.

Into the valley of death rode the twenty-three, I thought, as we headed back. Lovah reined her panther to my side.

"Remember one thing," she said as we rode, "your paavan is faster in every way than the okas they ride. It is our real advantage over them. You are riding, Lipso, a well-trained animal. I know because I trained him. Give him the reins if we meet danger. And stay close to me, because this will not be a contest of fists."

Lipso *was* well trained because when I leaned over and put my arms about Lovah's waist and drew her close, he didn't move an inch or slack his pace. I kissed her hard, perhaps not as satisfyingly as I wanted, but well enough for the situation. I guessed it was the first time she'd ever been kissed because she brought one hand to her mouth in wonder. The most beautiful smile I'd ever seen came to life on those wonderful lips and before I knew what she was intending, she had reached in my direction, hauled me to her and gave me a kiss in return. Years went by before I came out of the halo-like daze I was in.

The dirty dogs had set the whole place on fire. Not only that but there were some who were still alive in the inferno. We could hear the screams of the poor devils. Jimno took the lead as though he was born to it.

HIS hand shot up and we rode up until we were a narrow circle about him. He gestured with his hand toward a stretch of trail that would lead us between the usual lush jungle growth with which I was now familiar.

"It seems," Jimno said in a growling voice, "that they are too intent on loot, pillage and worse...to pursue. Or perhaps they think we will wait their coming on bended knees. But soon they will think of those who escaped. Then will they ride after us. There is no trail other than through there..."

Again I looked to the dense brush and narrow trail and immediately a picture formed in mind of what could happen were we to lay a trap.

"...We are few but enough for what we can do. To face them squarely would be suicidal. Rather let us pair off and infilter through the brush but not too far off the trail. Our paavans move like shadows between the narrowest part of the forest. Their clumsier and slower beasts cannot follow. Therefore let us make haste and make rendezvous with them as they enter and harry them until they reach the open spaces. Then, when we have done with them here, let us ride ahead and make sure we meet them again later, where the forest meets the hills..."

The women wore broad smiles long before he had finished. They needed nothing further in the way of command or instruction. Like shadows, they melted into the greyness that bordered the lush growth. In a few seconds it seemed as though there had never been human or beast on the trail. Jimno, one of the women warriors, Lovah and myself, were the last to lose ourselves in the dense growth.

"Give Lipso his head," Lovah said as she moved forward. "He has been trained to follow..."

We wound about, our beasts moving in complete silence, over fallen logs, between the boles of jungle-giants, which pressed so closely together that it seemed impossible anything other than a snake could maneuver his way through. Yet the lithe black bodies managed with an ease that astounded me. Deeper and further into the gloomy green we went. As though aware of the impending clash, the forest life was stilled, not even the birds trilling their songs.

Lipso and Lovah's mount moved tail to snout, so close were they. I watched the lithe form of the woman ahead. Suddenly her hand went to the scabbard and the long sword came into the open. I followed suit. I could see nothing. There *was* nothing to be seen. The jungle looked as impenetrable as ever. The sun never existed as far as I was concerned. We moved in an odorous and silent world. Then Lipso stopped and I became aware that Lovah was sitting erect and expectant.

From somewhere ahead there came a grunting and squealing. The sound of men's voices lifted in rough talk also came to our ears, but so dimly I couldn't make out the words. My throat tightened so that my breath came out in a wheeze when I realized that the moment was at hand for our ambush. There was but a single question in my mind. How were we going to go about it?

Lovah answered that question.

Her fingers pulled lightly on the reins and before my startled eyes her mount leaped nimbly up the huge bole of a nearby tree. Immediately, Lipso followed. I clung tightly with both hands about the panther's neck. The animals moved gingerly out on a limb, mine a little below and to the left of Lovah's. We perched thus for the space of perhaps thirty seconds. I saw that we were almost directly above the narrow, twisting trail. The grunting sounds of the animals and the guttural sounds of their riders came more distinctly to my ears.

They were telling each other, with a horrible relish, of what they had done, while the houses burned…

A PECULIAR series of tuneless whistles broke from the midst of the forest about us and simultaneously with those sounds the *how* of the ambush was made clear to me. I saw Lovah's thighs contract and grip close to the lean sides of the animal she was on. And the next second the panther was a black streak of silent fury falling through space. Nor was he alone. Only reflex came to my help, otherwise I would have ended up on my face in the grass-grown jungle-land. But my thighs did tighten and one arm managed to hold the reins, as Lipso left his feet in a leap after the first panther.

We leaped into the midst of some eight or nine mounted men. The lizard-elks animals they were on were squealing wildly as Lipso and the other beast leaped among them, slashing with claw and tearing with fang. The instant we reached the ground Lovah shouted for me to dismount. Now we were on our own. As I slashed wildly about with the razor-sharp sword, I heard the sounds of battle all about me. But so dense was the underbrush and so furious the action, so disconnected, I got only flashes. But one was unforgettable. Jimno had engaged the largest of the enemy, a man perhaps a foot taller than himself.

The single glimpse I caught was of Jimno being pressed back into the jungle by the power of the other's swordplay. Then they were lost to my sight. Nor was I interested any further. Death and I had come to grips. The sword in my hand was like a broom handle for all I knew of its use. And these men we had ambushed had been trained since childhood to its murderous use.

There was only one factor that saved me from instant extinction. We were fighting in brush. There simply wasn't room for fancy footwork and dexterous strokes. It was hack and chop and duck, and when it came to that I didn't have to take a back seat to anyone. A lifetime spent in ducking girls I'd promised things to came in use.

He got in the first chops, but I ducked and took a couple of whacks myself. All the time my brain was worrying about Lovah. After all, I was fighting one-on-one. She was taking on the rest. He came at me again, and this time I waited until he was a couple of feet from me, about the length of a sword stroke. The stroke I used was my favorite service stroke in tennis. I was a shade slow, but it was enough. He got his blade up in a parry. What happened to him should happen to the rest, I thought. Something strange had happened to Hank and myself in our journey from Earth to this place, our strength multiplied tenfold. My blade not only knocked his to one side but the end four inches sliced right through his collar bone and down into his chest. He let out a single screech and fell backward, blood fountaining out from the huge wound.

I wasted no time in sympathy. There were the ringing sounds of blade striking blade not far from me. I leaped over a fallen log and into the place where Lovah was battling. She had backed up so that she had her shoulders to a huge tree. Facing her were four men. Two others lay in the curious positions the dead assume.

MY APPROACH was silent. The first they knew of my presence was when one of them fell face forward. He fell straight down. He looked kind of funny, what with his head going one way and his body another. Nor did I waste time in watching him. Once again my tennis came to a more different use. I'd used a forehand on the first. The second fell into a backhand that would have been envied by any tennis pro. There was only one thing wrong with it. I clouted this character across the chest. The blade went all the way into him. And stuck there. I yanked at it and finally stuck one foot up against the guy and tried to pull it out, but no use. It wasn't until I thought of the dead man's own sword and turned and picked it off the ground that I realized that all the time I was vulnerable to attack from the other two.

I needn't have worried. They were being taken care of but good. My Lovah was no amateur with the sword. The two characters were doing an anxious tap dance to the tune she was playing. I'm sure they wanted to be anywhere else but where they were. Even as I watched she lunged with her sword straight out and caught one of them right through his throat.

"*Lovah!*" I screamed suddenly. "Watch it!"

She had slipped on a wet spot of grass and in that second the other one was at her side. Her sword had flown out of her hand as she threw up her arms trying to maintain her balance. She was completely helpless and I was too far from her to help. There was but one thing to do. I lifted my sword and heaved it, point forward. The guy's sword was already coming down when mine hit. It went all the way through him. He fell straight down over the girl. And from where I was standing it looked like I'd thrown too late.

"Lovah," I moaned as I ran forward and knelt at her side. I shoved the carcass of the goon who'd fallen over her to one side and lifted her up. "Angel! Talk to me…"

"I will," she said, "as soon as I get my breath back. Now," she continued after I'd kissed her for a while, "let us get out of here. They'll organize soon and we are too few to do more than we have…"

She arose and puckered her lips into that tuneless whistle. In a second the two panthers came trotting to us. Their snouts were stained with blood and it drooled from the corners of their mouths. Lovah leaped into the flat saddle and I followed. There was no need to give the animals their orders. They knew by instinct what was expected of them.

Whirling, they loped off at top speed through the thick growth. In a short while we joined the rest at the rendezvous agreed on. We took stock. Our entire losses were one warrior and two panthers. Jimno was elated.

"We have halted them for a while. Now they will proceed with caution which was our purpose... Let's turn about and make for the hills."

HANK had grim lines to his face. But they were erased at sight of me riding in the fore with Lovah and Jimno. Jimno shouted the news while we were still a hundred feet from the entire remnants of the camp. A wild yell of exultation went up from their throats at the news. Only Luria held her reserve. But even she could not help but smile.

They surrounded us and asked a hundred questions. I let Jimno take the stage. The guy deserved it. He had staged a masterful ambush and had gotten away with remarkably small losses. Hank dragged me to one side and pumped me dry of what had happened.

The sound of Luria's voice interrupted us.

"Let us not waste time in useless talk. Jimno and the others did a good job. They have delayed the pursuit for a time. But when they realize how small a force opposed them they will come the more quickly.

"We cannot stay here and we cannot go in a single body to the place where we will be safe. Therefore, I think it best to assign squad leaders to groups who will then take different trails to our eventual goal.

"Jimno, because you have proved your unquestioned leadership, you will take the largest group, all warriors, and fight a rear-guard action to delay and harass the enemy. Wamini and Saavah will lead the women and children by the trail I have outlined, to the place of safety. Lovah, you will be in charge of the balance of the warriors, all the women and all the men, who will wait here until Jimno returns, and fight a battle with the enemy. But that can wait until the others have left."

It was remarkable how little confusion there was. Luria amazed Hank and myself in her showing of leadership. It just didn't seem right that so beautiful a woman should have qualities that was rightfully man's. In a very short time several lines spread from the encampment in various directions, some toward the hills close by, others back in the direction from which we'd just come and one, the smallest group, in a direction at right angles to the back trail. This group was led by Jimno. I wondered where they were going. When the last group had left, only Hank, Luria, two of her personal guards, and myself were left.

"And now," Luria said turning to Hank and me, "we too must journey. Let us hope we are successful..."

"Why? Where are we going?" Hank asked.

"To the valley of the mists. To that same valley where first you saw me, as though in a dream. There, the Groana Bird makes his home, and there is where the dread beast of flame lives. We must bring back the Groana Bird..."

"Why?" Hank asked again.

"Because it was the symbol of my father's strength. And even Loko will respect it and give up his pretensions. Remember how you were captured? He too wants the bird. But we have one thing in our favor. I know the bird's haunts. He doesn't."

I listened to the first part of it. Then my thoughts wandered. Lovah had been chosen to give battle to the enemy. Suddenly I felt fear strike at my innards. I knew then, that I had fallen in love with my Amazon. And I was frightened. They had seemed so few, riding back toward what? Their doom?

"We have a long ride ahead, and a dangerous one," Luria continued. "Talk wastes time…"

CHAPTER EIGHT

IT WAS the longest ride I'd ever been on. Since there was no appreciable change in time, I never knew what was what. We slept, we ate, and we rode, and always the sun was overhead.

There were times for eating and sleeping and after a while I managed to gain a sort of idea from our sleeping habits of an approximate time. We were on the trail at least one week. The topography held to about the same character until about the last day.

On the first few miles of our ride, after the awakening on what I called the seventh day, we rode through a narrow valley set between two high and precipitous hills. We had been in the midst of mountain country for a long time. Suddenly Luria, who was riding at the head of our little column, waved her hand to the right and swerved from the path she'd been riding on to a narrow trail, which led straight up the wan of the cliff.

The trail straightened and to my horror became part of the wall itself. Even a Rocky Mountain goat would have found it difficult traveling. Not these panthers, though. They moved swiftly, and surely along the narrow trail. Then, with an abruptness that took my breath away, the trail ended against a barrier of rock. I was next to last so I could not see what Luria was doing or where she was going. I saw only the chalky-white face of the wall towering over us. Lipso had stopped and was waiting patiently to go on.

The panther and its mount directly in front of me began a slow advance and Lipso followed. I saw then where we were

155

heading and my wonder was boundless. A path had been hewed like a tunnel directly into the cliff. And for the first time I knew darkness on Pola.

It was instant. I don't know how the animals managed to find their way. Instinct, I suppose. But the darkness was too much for me. I couldn't see my nose in front of my face. And since our footfalls were muffled we seemed to be traveling in the silence of a tomb.

Once more the transition from dark to light was instantaneous. We were in a shallow amphitheater, but one which stretched for limitless distances. We rode up to join Luria. She looked out over the mists and said in a small childish voice:

"The valley of the mists, the lair of the beast. My father took me and Mokar here once in the long ago. Mokar has never forgotten. Look..."

We followed the line of her outstretched finger and an involuntary shiver shook my frame. Never had I seen a more forbidding place. The mists were like feathers of smoke. They filled the place in breadth, width and height. Now and then the mists would part for an instant and black damp rock would show monstrous shapes like a scene from Hell. Strange hissing noises came alive to lend added terror to the prospect. Luria's shoulders squared and turning to us, she said in dry, sure tones:

"We gain nothing standing here. The Groana bird lies in there. Let us be on our way. One thing—the beast of flame lies in wait. Watch for him."

There was but one trouble with being on our way. The instant we moved into the mists it was like stepping into a thick fog. I know I was riding alongside one of the two huge women who were Luria's personal guards. The next I knew, Lipso and I were alone in this strange and terrifying world.

Lipso sensed it immediately and his steps became cautious and slow. He snuffled loudly, nor was he alone. The rest of them also used their noses rather than their eyes. The mists would part now and then giving us glimpses of what lay beyond. It also permitted us to see whether we were still together. We weren't. Once I saw Hank. He looked a bit bewildered and his head was moving from side to side as though in search of Luria. The mists closed down and once more we groped our way through the fog.

I echoed in a minor chord the sudden scream that arose from the mists. It was a human scream. And hard on its heels came a roar that turned me cold with fear. Lipso grunted a low growl and his body tensed, the muscles bunching under me as though he was getting ready to spring.

Like magic the mists parted altogether and I saw the whole of this horrendous place. We were in a grotto. Directly in front of me was one of the women guards. By her side was Hank. I as usual was the last in the parade. Off to one side away from the rest was Luria. But all of us were looking at what lay in front of us.

IT WAS a nightmare. The body of the beast before us was a good thirty feet in length. I recognized it as the same in species as those we had encountered in the pit. But this one was the daddy of them all. Smoke and fire came from its nostrils. The great triangular head moved back and forth like a snake's. And lying under the ridiculous paws was the broken body of the other amazon…

"Back!" Luria shouted. "I'll take care of him."

Hank's shout was lost in the roar that came from the animal's throat. I was too terrified to move. I could only watch with fascinated horror at the spectacle that followed. Luria's guard must have come onto the cave that was the beast's lair unaware of its occupant. The panther she rode must have thrown her in its panic to escape, because she was lying face upward on her back. I saw too that the grotto was immense, the entrance being at least a hundred feet in height.

Then the mists closed in again.

Lovah's admonition came to mind. That if I was ever in a spot to give Lipso his head. I let the reins go slack and the shape below me moved back and forth in its tracks without making a forward step. When the beast did go forward it was slowly. A rank odor, so strong I had to hold my breath at intervals, wafted in to us from ahead. The roars had increased in both intensity and constancy. And now they were closer...

And again the mists lifted.

Lipso halted his progress. A snarl rose in his throat. The tableaux had evolved in action. Luria raced forward. Her lovely body was bent forward until it seemed to lie along the sleek black length of the panther, her spear was couched low, the long needle-tip pointed straight for the beast ahead. I saw her heels dig into Mokar's side. And with a ferocious roar, Mokar leaped forward.

I yelped in horror as Lipso followed Mokar's lead. There had been some sort of telepathic orders from either Mokar or his mistress. Because the beasts of Hank and the other guard also shot toward the beast in the grotto entrance. Luria reached the beast first though we couldn't have been more than ten feet behind. The last fifteen feet Mokar left his feet in a tremendous bound. The terror ahead rose on its hind legs, the tiny paws waving ridiculously toward the woman and her mount. But the terrible snout was open and, its rows of huge teeth an obstacle I never dreamt of having to face, were directed toward the foolhardy things challenging it.

At the very last second Mokar changed direction with a wondrously lithe movement of his body and instead of coming in from the front, came in from the side. Then Lipso was in the air too. Instinctively I brought my spear to a position similar to the one Luria had used.

A violent roar of rage shook the air. Luria had driven her spear straight into the leathery skin of the beast's throat. She hadn't waited for the thing to retaliate. Mokar had seen to it. His mission accomplished, Mokar turned tail and leaped to safety. But Lipso wasn't that fortunate.

I was a lot more clumsy than Luria had been. My spear glanced off the thick skin and flew to one side. My thoughts had been on the destructive power of the great teeth and jaws. I'd forgotten about his tail. Suddenly it swished around and caught Lipso full in the side. I heard him grunt softly and felt the beast below me go limp. I barely managed to fall to one side as Lipso was knocked a half dozen feet by the blow. He lay where he fell, nor did he so much as move a muscle.

Now the *thing* had something it could vent its wrath on. I managed to get to my feet just as the beast reached me. I had been given a sword. I drew it just as I felt the beast's rank breath on my face and saw the saw-teeth within a foot of me. I leaped to one side, and as I did, swung the long blade.

THE sword went right through the ugly snout. The most frightful roar of all went up and a thick terribly odorous mucous flowed out of the wound in a torrent. The stench of it was overpowering. There was a confused sound of shouting as I backed off a couple of feet. But I was strictly intent on the *thing* in front of me. It hadn't given up the battle. It still had a tail and too obviously no intelligence. Though the wound I had given it was terrible, the beast seemed unaware of it. Its tail swished out again but this time I was on the watch for it. And this time I wasn't alone.

Hank's voice was low but full of strength:

"Okay, pal. Let's go to work."

This time it was we who attacked.

Hank took one side and I the other. We leaped in, our swords swinging with perhaps not the finesse of the others, but certainly with better effect. For every time we struck, the steel plowed right through. Either the thickness of skin was deceptive, or our strength was greater than we had ever imagined it to be. The whole slaughter couldn't have taken more than a few seconds. The last of the pieces to be dissected was the tail. Two swipes, one a forehand the other a backhand, and the tail was just a memory.

In the meantime the other guard had joined us. Her first thrust with the spear had been a good one. She had managed to withdraw the weapon before her paavan leaped to safety. Now she stood by our side and jabbed with it like a probing needle. I wondered why until quite suddenly the beast sank down and rolled slowly over. The *thing* had a spot through which he could be dealt a mortal bow. The gal did it with one jab.

We stopped our swinging and stood looking at each other, our breaths coming in shallow gasps. The woman towered over us and had the muscles of a foundry worker. She shook her head in admiration and said:

"Truly, you two are the greatest warriors in all Pola. Never have I seen such sword strokes. Never have I seen such strength. The Habasi is not faced calmly. And this one is truly the largest I have ever seen. His skin is like the thick bark of the Ofas tree, which is like a metal. Yet your blades sliced him as though he were meat ready for the table..."

She continued to shake her head in wordless admiration. I noticed that Hank, however, was no longer basking in the glow of that admiration. His head was bent to one side. Suddenly he snapped the fingers of his free hand and whirled to me.

"Luria! Where is she?"

The mists seemed to have lifted some. They no longer enveloped us with their foggy, tenuous fingers. There was nothing to be seen of Luria or Mokar.

The wide nostrils of the woman spread in anger. She bent in a semi-crouch, as though she were sniffing a danger not to be seen. Hank, too, kept looking from one side of the tortured bit of ground as though he thought the girl had fallen among some of the rocks. As usual, when it came to Luria, Hank was the first to guess at her whereabouts. He gathered she hadn't fled the scene. He must have also reasoned then that there was but one place she could be, the grotto that had been the Habasi's home.

Without a word or a look, Hank whirled and leaped toward the entrance. I followed but not with as much enthusiasm. In fact the woman was on Hank's heels. There was a dim light as we came into the grotto proper. It died slowly until we were running in total darkness after the first few hundred feet. Suddenly, as though someone had turned on dim lights all over the cave, a radiance came to life. It wasn't much but it was enough to light our way.

WE WERE running on some sort of moss, for our footsteps were soundless. The cave was dry and rather cool. It led straight back and at a slightly downward grade. Suddenly we came against a blank wall. There were no forks in the road we had been running. The cave just ended up against solid rock.

"What the…" Hank growled. "But this doesn't make sense."

"Does anything in this goofy place?" I asked.

"Then where did Luria go?" he asked.

In the meantime the woman had been moving along the wall. Suddenly she bent and began a loud sniffling some two feet from the ground.

"Mokar," she announced, "has been here. His scent is strong here…"

Hank took her at her word. But me, I was skeptical.

"Well," I ventured, "then the only conclusion is that she vanished into thin air. And knowing the young lady as well as we do, I wouldn't doubt it."

"Uh-uh," Hank said, shaking his head doggedly. "There wouldn't be any reason for it."

"No? Perhaps her old man was a smart guy and put this Groana Bird in a location where only his daughter could get at it."

"Then why did he keep it a secret?" Hank asked.

I had no answer for that.

In the meantime the woman had been busy. Her fingers tapped the surface, ran lightly across the face, as though in search of some crack not seen by the eyes. Suddenly she let out a bark of triumph. We stepped quickly to her side.

"What's up?" I asked.

For an answer she slammed the palm of her hand against the rock. It spun away from her and before our astonished eyes we saw a long narrow room, high-ceilinged and with walls of natural rock. At the far end we saw Mokar lolling at his ease. Of Luria, nothing was to be seen. Of course we realized what had happened. The wall swung on a pivot. Luria's bodyguard's sense of smell had told her that Mokar had come to that point. Unless they *had* disappeared into air, they had to be somewhere beyond the wall.

Hank was first to step through. I followed and the woman brought up the rear. We saw it simultaneously. In one corner of the room was an immense bird cage. Luria stood beside it crooning something to a brilliantly colored bird, which rocked back and forth on a perch. She turned, saw us, smiled a welcome, and turned back to the bird. We came over and ranged ourselves beside the girl. I looked at the bird with curiosity.

They could call it what they wanted, Groana Bird, holy bird, or anything else. As far as I was concerned it was a polly. Hank had the same sentiments.

"A cockatoo," he said in a low voice.

"Aah, shut up," the bird suddenly screeched.

"Shut up yourself," Hank blazed.

"Okay, if that's what you want," the bird said.

Luria turned an angry face to us.

"And just when I had soothed the Groana Bird," she said through slitted lips. "I could, I could…" her voice trailed off in helpless syllables.

"Groana, Shmoana," I said. "What is this? He's nothing but a parrot. What's all the fuss about?"

"Yeah," the parrot said. "What's all the fuss for?"

Hank and I were both stunned that the bird was speaking in what appeared to be common American vernacular.

"What in the hell…" I said, a look of total puzzlement on my face.

"Do you mean," Hank asked, "that this is the holy bird your father held in such high esteem?"

"The wisest animal in the whole world," Luria said. "What he says becomes law. We must bring him back with us."

"So okay," I said. "Only let's get out of this dungeon. It's beginning to give me the creeps."

We began searching for the door to open the cage and discovered there was none. The bars were set close enough to hold the bird prisoner. I wondered how he had originally been placed inside. The bird watched our parade around his cage with cocked head and jaundiced eye. After a few moments, he broke out in his raucous voice:

"I'm getting hungry. Let's get me out of this place."

"I'd like to twist that fool head of yours from those feathers," I said viciously.

"Ha-ha!" the bird crowed. "So would a lot of them. So come and get me…"

I SAW red then. I saw a lot of other colors, all on the bird, and I had a wild desire to tear the bird in two. I stalked forward, grabbed the bars and twisted, even though I knew I was being foolish. After all, even I could see they were made to hold something a lot stronger than a bird. But I was mad…

They bent as though they were made of spaghetti. There was a last raucous crow of delight, a flash of color past my eyes and the voice of the bird behind me:

"Thanks, pal. I was getting tired of being a bird in a cage."

I whipped around and there was our little feathered friend perched on the shoulder of Luria. I was still annoyed. I gave him a fiendish look (I hoped) and stalked toward the two of them. Luckily, Hank stopped me.

"Aah, let 'im come," the bird said. "I'll tear 'im in two, or three. I got lots of numbers."

"But only one life, bird. You ain't a cat. Just remember that," I mumbled darkly.

The parrot cocked his head to one side, gave Luria a sidelong look from his bright eyes and said:

"Where'd you find the squares, beautiful? What dopes! Especially the one who talks."

"Oh, Groana Bird," Luria said. "We have searched long for you. The days are dark on Pola since my father left to join his soul mates…"

That blasted bit of feathers and beak just couldn't keep quiet.

"That's what I kept tellin' the old boy. Better watch your knittin' or they're gonna take that sweater apart before you're through with it. So he perled when he shoulda knit and see what happened. But like yap-jaw says, this dungeon's beginning to give me the creeps. And I've been here a lot longer than he. So…"

Luria's sigh of happiness, as she turned and started back, was like a song to Hank. He stepped close to her side and looked down at her with a grin that, had it been wider, would have set his ears on the other side of his head. Oh, well, I thought, now that the worst is over and we haven't got anything else to do except pick up the marbles, maybe she'll send us back and I can finish that story for Fa…

CHAPTER NINE

THEY whistled up the dead woman's paavan for me, and with the bird still perched on Luria's shoulder, we started on the way back. Once more we moved through the valley of the mists but this time the terror was gone. Again we came to the tortuous path along the shoulder of the steep mountain side. And this time, like with all dangers circumvented, it seemed not quite so frightening. I even found myself whistling as the sleek, sure-footed panthers trotted along. We passed a twisted tree I remembered was not far from where we'd come off the main trail. And in a very short while we were on the broad trail leading back to Gayno.

At ease now, I noticed things that had escaped me before. To our right some hundred yards, a wide river followed a winding path, and now and then I could see the swirling muddy waters. To our left the grass grew thick and rank, sometimes higher than a paavan's shoulder. I remembered how the women rose from the midst of grass like this and thought what an excellent ambush it would make. We were running on what I called a path. I called it that for want of another name. Really it was just a flattened area among the other grasses.

Soon we came to the short bit of parkland that, once traversed, would lead us to the wider path back to Gayno. The path wound among the trees for perhaps a mile. Then we saw open reaches and shortly the trees thinned and we were racing in the open again. A soft wind ruffled my hair, the air was not too warm and the sun held a brightness that, unlike Earth's, did not irritate. For the first time in this strange land I felt peace. But not for long.

THERE must have been a thousand of them. They descended on us like flies. Luria was the first to see them. Some sixth sense warned her of their proximity, for suddenly she drew Mokar up sharp, raised a hand on high as a signal to halt, and as the ambush rose about us, shouted a warning. But it was of no avail.

We had been running with some five yards between each rider. There was no chance to get to Luria. I found myself surrounded by dozens of Loko's men. I glimpsed Captain Mita up ahead close to Luria. Then hands were reaching for my bridle. I had no chance to get my sword out but my fists weren't tied down. I must have knocked ten of them silly before someone thought to use the hilt of a sword on my noggin. I saw more stars than the heavens held, and in a twinkling the darkness of unconsciousness.

I was jostled about. My head rocked from side to side like someone was using it for a metronome. I was strapped to what was undoubtedly the worst smelling man in all of Pola. His stench was nearly unbearable. I peered through bleary eyes at a long line of warriors strung out ahead of us. I managed to turn my head and saw that the line behind us was almost as long.

There was someone ahead swearing a blue streak. I couldn't make the words out but it didn't take long for me to recognize the voice. Good old Groana! He was telling them a thing or two. A lot of good it was doing, I thought. This time we wouldn't get off so easy. What was more, Loko had Luria now. I began to wonder what he wanted of her.

We came to a fork in the road and turned right. After a while we came to a broad meadowland. Tents had been set up in well-laid sections like streets or, suddenly I knew what, a military encampment. To our right as we entered, was a stockade where I saw a huge number of the strange beasts they used. Sentries were posted every few yards. Their discipline was excellent. The warriors deployed to their respective areas, leaving some ten to guard us as we followed Captain Mita, the giant who had slapped me around, and Loko. We drew up before the most pretentious of the tents. This proved to be Loko's personal quarters.

They had to cut me loose from the guy I was with and whoever did the cutting didn't care whether or not he got some skin with it. In fact he laughed heartily as I yelped more than once when the sword drew blood. But the moment I was on my feet all merriment ceased. The point of the man's sword tickled my spine all the way into the shady confines of the tent.

The furnishings were simple: a couple of easy chairs of good design, with cushions for seats; several benches of plain wood, and a dozen low hassocks scattered about served for seats. The back wall of the tent was guarded by five men and a like number of women-warriors. They stood stiffly at attention, spears held firmly in one hand while the other was at their hip in readiness to grab at the sword if needed.

Loko and the big guy found seats side by side at the far end of the tent. Loko grunted tiredly and said:

"My years are too many for these strenuous doings. Ye have given me a merry chase. Perhaps it was well that ye escaped the pit. For surely we would not have found our quarry so easily. And better, the prize she carried. Ho, guard, bring the holy bird to me..."

WE WERE standing in a close group, Hank, Luria, her guard and myself. The bird was still perched on Luria's shoulder. We had been stripped of weapons. As the guard stepped to Luria's side Hank took a single step forward and knocked the character right on his seat.

"Atta boy. Hit 'im one for me," the Groana shouted raucously. "Kick 'im in the slats."

Loko's voice was low, seemingly without anger, yet I felt a shiver:

"Ye have used force before. Shall we be compelled to answer in the same?"

"No!" Luria's answer was a clarion call. "Enough of force. For hundreds of years Pola has known nothing else. You decry the use of it yet never feel any compunctions about using it when it avails you best. By my father's name I swear the bird will avail you nought. There are other means of freeing Pola from your tyranny."

I wanted to cheer. I felt an admiration for Luria. She was all right.

The big guy up there with Loko thought so too. He let out a wordless bellow and rose to his feet.

"By the Groana Bird!" he shouted. "Loko. Your word. I want that woman, hear me?"

"Over my dead body!" came the answer from my side. It was Hank. Good old Hank and his good old big mouth. Wasn't he ever going to learn to keep it closed? He got the only reply the other character could have given.

"I shall be only too glad to arrange that," the big fellow said.

"Enough, Wost!" Loko broke in. "Brawls are for those in their cups. Save it for then. Now then, enough of this. Bring the bird up here."

This time no one raised either fist or voice when two of the guards stepped out and took the bird from Luria's shoulder. The one who was carrying the bird carried it gingerly and when he got to Loko handed it to the old man

169

with fingers that shook palpably. There was the strangest look of triumph on Loko's face as he got the bird.

"Now," and this time his voice was raised in ecstasy, "now *I* shall rule. By the sign of the Holy Groana Bird. By the sign of his feathers, by the sign of his wisdom and by the sign of my possession…"

"Aah, nuts," said the parrot unexpectedly.

"Holy Bird," Loko said in tones of awe, as though the goofy parrot had said something beyond his comprehension, "say more in your infinite wisdom."

"Is this character square?" the bird asked. "Why don't he get the score straight? Boy, oh boy! How did this oldy get dealt in?"

"I don't know," I said. "Maybe you can arrange his getting dealt out?"

"That's all right with me, allreeti, allreeti," Groana said.

LOKO kept shifting his glance from the bird to me and back again as we carried on. His fingers tapped nervously together in constant motion and his brow showed irritable corrugations in his effort to understand.

"What does he say?" Loko asked me in petulant tones.

"The Holy Bird says," I began as portentously as I could, "that he is weary and needs rest."

"But of course," Loko made haste to fall in to the suggestion. "May he forgive an old man's stupidity. Many, many years have passed in his incarceration. May the memory of the man who enslaved him become dust in our mouths, a stench in our nostrils."

"Gadzooks!" Groana said. "The varlet needs a cup to wander in. 'Pon my soul! An' by my Lud Harry, with whom I spent many a roistering night, get him one and fill it with the dregs of the grape so that Merry England shall have peace this day."

"Peace? Peace?" Loko said. "He desires peace?"

"Aah! Shut up!" the bird said and bent and nipped Loko on the lobe of the nearest ear.

"He means quiet," I said. "And if I am allowed a word...?"

Loko held one hand to his wounded ear and said:

"Say on..."

I decided that formality was the note to strike. Loko liked it well:

"The Holy Bird has some small affection for the girl. Since it is obvious she cannot escape, perhaps it were best that he stay with her."

"No! I do not trust her. Further, she is, as are the rest of you, my prisoners. I have as yet not decided the disposition I intend of ye."

"'Tis a sorry day f'r the Irish, me lad," Groana said. "An' sure an' if it's the last act of me life I'll kiss the Blarney Stone on me hands and knees but let me have a chance at a shillalah..."

"You see, Loko," I said in triumph, "another word, a single syllable of denial to his desires, and he promises to call on the holy Blarney Stone. Believe me. Woe betide anyone accursed by the Stone."

Loko blanched to the color of wet ivory at the words. The only one of the three, Loko, Mita and Wost, who showed no alarm at the words, was Wost. But he was probably too dull-witted to know fear.

"But of course, of course the Holy Bird can stay with the girl," Loko said quickly. "I was but thinking of its security."

"Is that schmoe kidding?" Groana asked.

"What does he say? What does he say?" Loko asked. He was like a kid before a microphone without a quizmaster.

"He says he's tired and wants to rest," I said.

"Assuredly. Assuredly," Loko said, shaking hands and head at the same time. "The time for sleep has come. Captain Mita, escort the prisoners."

"Guests might be a better word," I said, being brave all of a sudden.

For the first time Loko showed anger. His eyes blazed for an instant, then hid themselves behind hooded lids. His voice held an icy edge when he said:

"Prisoners… Do not try my patience…"

I shrugged my shoulders in a gesture of bravery I certainly didn't feel. I *knew* I was shaking, quivering in fear, yet somehow, I managed to say in quite normal tones:

"Okay. Let it be like you say. Only let's stop with all this talk. I said the bird was tired. Do we have to talk some more about that?"

"Take them to their quarters," Loko bit out.

Captain Mita and his men played escort. It was just to another tent, one not too far from Loko's. There was no question, however, that we were going to be prisoners. Mita posted enough guards around the tent to guard an army. They stood shoulder to shoulder in a huge square, and within that square another, also shoulder to shoulder.

This tent didn't have the accommodations Loko's had. It was not to be expected. But there were several cushions. Luria and her personal guard took those. I hid a smile. Here were a couple of dames who were doing their best to act like men yet used a woman's prerogative immediately as the chance presented itself. Hank and I found the ground hard but not too much so.

Very soon after we made ourselves comfortable, the feeling for sleep manifested itself. It was a strange thing, this feeling for sleep. There was no night or day on Pola since the sun shone all the time. And the business of sleep was as regulated an affair as though there had been passed a law about it. One's eyes became heavy, one's every muscle felt an odd relaxing, and very soon afterward one simply relaxed somewhere and went to sleep.

The strangest part of it all was that sleep was instantaneous all over Pola. It was not up to the individual as to when he slept. When one slept, all slept.

AWAKENING, too, took place simultaneously. I yawned once or twice, arose and stretched and looked at the others. The parrot blinked its eyes, cocked its head and said:

"Well, bless our little... Say! how's about putting on the feed bag, kids?"

Luria and the other woman looked to me. And I suddenly became aware that I had been relegated to the parrot's interpreter. Not that Hank couldn't understand, but I had assumed that position in Loko's headquarters. I wasn't too happy about it. But I wasn't in any position to do anything about it now.

"He just wants to eat," I said sourly.

"Something wrong in that?" the bird asked. "Or am I supposed to live on air?"

"Don't get so fussy," I said. "How did you manage in that cave?"

"It was like this, short, dark and ugly," the bird said. "Believe it or not, I was in a trance."

"So put yourself back in a trance again, and forget about feeding that ugly face of yours," I said.

I ducked just in time. Before the last word had left my lips, Luria leaped for me. She swung a little late. Hank got there before she could swing again. She was white-faced in anger.

"I listened to him berate the Holy Bird yesterday and could barely contain my anger. I did so because he is your friend. But I can no longer contain my anger."

"Daughter...Daughter..."

We all looked to the parrot, who at Luria's sudden move had hopped to the hassock for safety. He was using a new voice now. Low, deep, flexible, it was a caressing voice, yet not a weak one. It brought Luria up short. I heard her whisper, "Father." Then the bird was talking again:

"Have all my teachings been in vain? Is anger the only vessel of those which I had placed at your disposal, the one to be used? Anger blinds one's senses, disturbs the delicate balance of reason, and as I once said, should only be used as a dart is used, for purposes of irritation.

"Surely is your predicament great. Surely is the hand of the traitor, Loko, heavy on your shoulders. He seeks the enslavement of all Pola, yet in your womanly manner you seek quarrels. Bend all your energies to the frustration of his desires and ambitions. Use these two whom you have brought from another plane of time and space to your help. Waste not their uses in arguments. Once I taught you the eyes, ears, nostrils, and all other physical senses can be tamed and put to the purpose for which they were intended. How little understanding was given to my teachings..."

"No, father!" Luria breathed sharply. "No..."

"Perhaps. But had you been alert in all your being, surely you would have understood the badinage between this man and myself. Silence would have been my weapon had I been displeased. But I think altogether, that perhaps the true reason for your lack of understanding lies in your having forgotten something I once said in your hearing.

"Daughter. Do you remember a day you walked into a council meeting? You sat at my feet and heard me tell them about the Holy Groana Bird. It was the first you heard of it. It was also the first they heard of it. I told them that in this bird was all the wisdom, past, present and future. Then, as you sat and watched I called for a slave to bring the bird forth. They marveled at the strange creature, for never had they seen one with such plumage. That very afternoon I spoke to you about transmigrations of bodies in space and time. You were old enough, wise enough and learned enough even then to add together the ingredients and come to the proper conclusion.

"For why, you should have asked, has there never been another such bird found? And how is it possible that this bird alone, of all the feathered beings in the world, is possessed of so much wisdom? I thought you understood. I was wrong. However, that is in the past. The present is bleak indeed. Therefore let us speak of the future. Loko has naught but ill in his bosom for all of you. Death lies across the threshold. How shall we circumvent him?"

CHAPTER TEN

LITTLE by little as the bird continued with his talk, we had drawn up close around him. We were a very tight circle about the hassock on which he stood perched.

"Daughter. Many years were spent in the teaching of the paavan I gave you. Mokar has the instincts of a wild animal. But he has been taught reason. Almost to the capacity of a human. He, as well as the mounts of Loko's minions, is in the stockade at the beginning of the encampment. Send a thought wave to him. Tell him to escape and bring the rescuers to us…"

I glanced over my shoulder and saw that Luria had her eyes closed. In a second she opened them and smiled. She shook her head as though she had followed her father's instructions.

"…Then let us wait as best we can for the coming of Jimno and the others. For I think Loko has thought over the arguments of your friend and has decided it would be best if I was with him."

The bird must have been psychic. The words were scarcely out of his mouth when the tent flaps were thrown back and Mita entered at the head of a squad of men. Without a word he marched up and swept his hand down and grabbed up the bird. The bird let out a frightened squawk, but before he could utter another sound Mita drew a hood from his belt and threw it over the parrot's head. In the meantime his squad stood guard with drawn swords over us. We had no chance to do anything about it.

"Tell Loko," Luria said as Mita was about to leave, "that it will do him no good. The Holy Bird has a will of its own…"

Mita smiled craftily.

"I do not doubt that," he said softly. But it is only a bird. If none but Loko hears the pearls of wisdom from its lips who will deny them?"

"I will," Luria said stoutly.

"A carcass has no voice or reason," Mita said. He grunted softly at the startled looks on our faces, then left.

"Why, those dirty, dirty…" Hank snarled and became silent for fear that his words would offend their ears.

But I was way ahead of them. So that was Loko's game. I had to admire the old character's shrewdness. All he had to do was slit the bird's tongue. Then who was there to say that Loko hadn't heard what he said he did? The bird wasn't going to be able to talk for itself. And we weren't going to be in any position, at least not until the dead can be resurrected, to be able to deny what Loko said.

Hank was pounding a fist into a palm. His grey-green eyes were bleak, and his face had that stony look of intense anger. I could almost read his mind. Evidently Luria also could.

"There's no use in empty and useless speculations or threats," she said. "We are helpless until help arrives. So let us be of good cheer."

"But how do you know help will come?" Hank asked.

She smiled and I thought of the Mona Lisa. "Mokar will not fail us," she said.

"Mokar…?"

"He is well on his way."

"But that stockade," Hank said.

"How was he able to…? But of course," understanding came to him, "I only hope he will make it in time. I think Loko won't give us too much of that commodity."

I stuck my two cents in and said, "And Loko's just the sort of guy who'd keep us on tenterhooks, draw the time out, let us think that maybe he won't cut our throats or whatever they're going to do, until the last second. Somehow, though, I have an idea that it won't be too soon."

A deep sigh turned our attention to the gigantic woman who was standing by Luria's side.

"What's wrong, Sanda?" Luria asked.

"I'm hungry," was the simple reply.

"The big gal talks sense," I said. "So am I."

BUT food wasn't to come for a long time. We sat around, lay around, talked, kept quiet, did everything to make the time pass more quickly. Luria and Hank got together in a corner and found things in common. I gathered, without being told, that Hank was wooing her and from the look on her face she wasn't finding it hard to take. But me, I was lost. The other member of our party was built along the lines of an overweight wrestler. Besides, she was a little short on the gray matter. About all there was for me was some silent philosophy. And that was pretty difficult to do in my position.

When food did come there was enough of it to feed an army.

"Like we'd asked for a last meal," Hank said.

I was taking a bite on something that tasted pretty good. But at those words I kind of lost my appetite.

"Why don't you gag yourself?" I asked.

"How about you doing it?" he wanted to know.

"I got both hands busy, dope," I said.

"So why don't you try eating with your feet? Ten fingers aren't enough for you."

"Look, sponge-head," I began edgily. I didn't like the tone of his voice. "I didn't ask to come along on the ride. So don't play Sad-Sack for my benefit…"

"Oh hell, Berk," he said. "I'm sorry."

"Don't be square," I said quickly. "That was *no* joke, son."

The two women kept giving us wondering glances. Luria could understand the King's English, but our version was over her head. The other gal was just size, no quality, except in muscle, of course. Suddenly the thought came to me how to make time pass. Talk, I had discovered long ago, is the finest devourer of time.

"Y'know," I said, "I've always been curious as to *how* you managed this business of, now I'm here, now I'm not. Just how do you do it?"

Tiny furrows formed between her eyebrows as she concentrated in an explanation which would be simple enough, yet explanatory:

"Oddly enough," she said, "it's a great deal more simple than you would imagine. Yet in one sense, more complex. You see, the whole thing is a matter of, shall we say, mind over matter…"

"So you said and you're glad," I broke in. "Elucidate on this bit of mental gymnastics."

"…But because it is mind triumphing over matter, the explanation is far more difficult than, say, the process of digestion," she went on as though there hadn't been an interruption.

"*Now* I understand," I said. "How simple the whole thing is, dear. But you're *so* clever…"

"Let her be, Berk," Hank said. "Go on, baby."

"Baby?" The word wasn't new to her but its connotation in the sense Hank gave, was.

"A term of endearment," I said. "But as Hank says, go on."

"Yes-s... Well. I simply *think* the object or person into another dimension of space and time. And that is the whole thing put as simply as I can."

"Fine. I *don't* get it! Tell me this now. When we first saw you, you were dressed in clothes very much the same as the women wear on our planet. How'd you do that?"

"I realized the instant the transposition took place, and I saw the manner of dress of your women, that I would be taken for a stranger. Not knowing the customs of your planet or country, I knew I had to do something about it. So naturally I..."

NOW wasn't that like a woman, I thought. Give her a joke to tell and she's a cinch to forget the punch line; give her a story and at the most interesting part she'll get that far-away look like as if she'd just remembered something she saw in a blouse and couldn't quite remember the shop. It was Hank, however, who nudged her on:

"So you what?"

"I lost my material self," she said.

I thought I heard right. But I wanted to make sure:

"What do you mean?"

"I mean I was no longer flesh and blood. For example, the outfit I wore. I got that from a shop on a city avenue. I remember it was dark and I simply walked in through the masonry and glass, took the outfit I wanted, and left. It was not the time for sleep so I walked about. I also remember an experiment I performed. This disappearance of material self was new to me. There was a man coming toward me. I walked straight at and through him. I remember it so well because he was with a woman and they were holding a conversation. He did not lose a word as I stepped through him."

So there *were* ghosts. They all come from Pola. Hmmm. Could that mean there was no Heaven, no Hell, just Pola? Aah…what was I thinking? Hank, it developed, wasn't thinking what I was.

"How simple it all is," he said. "All you have to do is dematerialize, step through the tent and escape."

"I thought of that and…No. We are all in this together. So we'll remain."

"But Loko will put you to death," Hank pointed out.

"When that bridge is on us we'll think about the crossing. Let us wait to see what Mokar brings."

"I don't know what he's bringing," I said. "But I hope he makes it fast. My patience is running out."

"Then you'll have to renew it," Luria said sharply. "Mokar might have come to Jimno in the midst of an engagement. What's more, they have to be certain that the children are in a safe place; that there will be enough guards; then they must locate Lovah and her force…"

"Lovah? Coming here?" I asked.

"But of course. Jimno's forces will not be enough."

The whole situation was bathed in a new light. I was a light-hearted Joe, ready for a lark or a wrestle, but now that my Lovah-honey was going to be involved—well! Things were shaping up. And not to my liking, either.

I said, "But even with Lovah's warriors there won't be enough to make a decent fight."

"It will be a combination of several factors," she pointed out. "In the first place there will be the element of surprise; secondly, Jimno and Lovah will not attack from the same direction; and thirdly, there is the factor of the paavans…"

I asked what they had to do with it.

"They were bred not for riding alone. Wait," she promised. "You will see how terrible they can be."

Hank got to whispering to her again so I sat in my little corner and digested what she told me. Maybe we had a chance. Then I got to thinking of the parrot and how she was going to manage to get him out of Loko's clutches. Hang it! I kept thinking of the bird as a material being. It was Luria's father, of course. Then I thought how silly that was, especially if one said it aloud. Then I stopped thinking.

Again time marched on. Suddenly I saw Luria place her hand to Hank's lips. He stopped talking and I stopped dreaming. She had heard something, something to which our Earthly ears were not attuned. She arose with a movement akin to one of her paavans, she rose lithely and stepped toward the tent opening. The rest of us followed suit.

"They come," she whispered. "I hear them in my mind. I don't know their plans, so be prepared for anything."

SHE warned us. But what happened was the last thing I thought would happen…

Fire arrows!

There must have been hundreds of them. They fell with tiny hissing sounds and whatever they touched burst into flame. In an instant the entire compound was a mass of fire and smoke. But we didn't wait to see what was going to happen next—not us. We got the hell out of there.

A torment of sound stuck our eardrums as we hit the open air. There were the terror-stricken sounds of men and women caught in the inferno, and above those were the horrible screams of animals tied to stakes and unable to escape. A pungent acrid odor came to my nostrils, an odor hard to place until I brought to mind a roast that had become too well-done.

I was just standing, listening openmouthed to the horror around me, when I heard a wild scream of exultation almost in my right ear. I pivoted and saw Luria, her face transfigured, looking straight down the avenue formed by the rows of tents. I understood her cry of triumph when I saw what was sweeping down the avenue. Mokar, riderless, was in the lead and directly behind him was Lovah and Jimno riding neck and neck in a wild race to get to us first.

Mokar paused only long enough for Luria to mount and get Hank up behind her and then, headed straight for the center tent, Loko's quarters. Lovah, looking like one of the Valkerie, only prettier, paused long enough for me to get on behind, then she was off after her queen. She handed me one of the two swords she held clenched in each of her dainty though dangerous fists.

She raised hers on high and screamed:

"For the Queen! Death to Loko and his!"

But it wasn't quite that easy. Captain Mita and the giant were no stupes. They were caught flat-footed, shocked with surprise, but it didn't last long—only long enough for them to start a dispersal of their forces. And the first thing they did, as though they realized the whole purpose of the attack, was to ring Loko's tent with guards. We rode, like the six hundred, into the jaws of death.

I don't know how many Luria had at her disposal; I had no chance to count even if I had wanted to, but certainly they weren't many. We hit the outer shell of the ring with the force of a battering ram, broke through and were swallowed by the inner rings. And those warriors were tough! Loko hadn't picked them for their kindness to their fellow-beings.

By some grim quirk of fate, Loko's tent was one of several the fire-arrows had missed. All around us the other tents blazed in fury. I caught a quick glimpse of them, then had no time for anything but the defense of my life and Lovah's too. Her arm was swinging a death tune to whoever was within reach of that terrible plaything. As for me, I was also swinging, maybe not with the assurance or ease of Lovah, but with as terrible effect. As I said before, I had discovered a strange thing about Pola, my strength was multiplied ten-fold for some reason, and though I did not always hit a vulnerable spot, the power of my blow when it did land was enough to decide the issue immediately.

But there was only one of me and Hank. The sheer weight of their numbers, plus the addition of reinforcements that kept arriving, lost us the encounter. A shrill whistling sound was suddenly heard and Lovah's face turned to mine with a dismal look of despair on it. I heard her words:

"Retreat! Luria calls retreat…"

THEN her mount's head was turned and we were racing like the wind back down the avenue of tents for the open ground beyond. We raced into the flat and kept running. I kept turning my head and saw Jimno. My heart leaped in my throat in sudden terror. I couldn't spot Hank or the girl. My pulse raced in time to the bounding paces of Lovah's paavan when I saw them at last. They were the last two out of the compound. Like a true queen, Luria had waited till the last of her subjects were away before she retreated.

We continued running at top speed for quite some time. As we raced onward endlessly, Lovah gave me an account of what had happened:

"Jimno is wonderful. A born leader. He caught the rear guards who had been left in town flat-footed. They hadn't a chance, and we mashed them to bits. Then we did an about face, ran in different directions, met at the rendezvous and made for the groups that we knew would be scouring the countryside for us. One by one we smashed them until at the end they were forced to join together. That was the moment for the third part of our forces to strike. The enemy was tired; we had fought them to a stand-still, and when the fresh forces attacked, they fled. Only to be met," she ended proudly, "by the paavans we let loose. Ahhh! The terror and destruction our wondrous paavans meted out!"

I could well imagine. I'd seen the gigantic panthers at work only a short while before, and what they could do to human flesh was not pretty.

She went on:

"...But we were still too few. Loko must have enlisted the aid of every warrior on Pola. More and more kept coming. Their sheer numbers would have won any pitched battle. We had to let off finally. Then came the message from our Queen..."

I looked from side to side and tried to gauge how many there were of us. It couldn't be done. We were strung out in a long line and since we were running in a flat—which reminded me of a prairie in a midwestern state—many of them were out of sight in the hip-high grass.

"Are we retreating to some plan?" I asked.

"Yes. The Great Forest lies ahead. Not even the bravest of all the warriors on Pola would dare venture in its depths. Ambush is only a matter of hiding behind a tree. Loko isn't that big a fool."

CHAPTER ELEVEN

AFTER a while Luria's forces merged until we were no longer stretched out in a long line although we were still riding loosely in groups of ten or twelve. Both Luria and Jimno rode their mounts close so that the three of our paavans were running abreast.

Luria seemed dispirited. Hank had his mouth close to her ear and I could see he was trying to break her mood. Maybe I know more about dames than Hank does. At any rate I put my two cents in.

"Cheer up, kid," I said. "We haven't lost yet…"

"We *won't* lose at all!" she said. "I wasn't thinking of how the battle stands. It's, it's…"

I divined her worry—that silly bird. To her it wasn't silly at all. It was her *father…* I kind of grinned and she noticed it.

"He smiles," she said grimly. "He is more brave even than I thought. The moment is dark and your friend smiles, Hank. He is a man."

"He's a damn fool," Hank said. But his eyes were twinkling in fondness (Henry Fondness, I called him) and he said, "He just doesn't know when to worry."

"The only thing I worry about is meeting a deadline for Ray Palmer," I replied. "But that wasn't what I was thinking about. I think I know what's bothering our pretty Queen. The bird…yes?"

She turned her head in surprise.

"Aha…I was right," I said, smiling a little. "Well, I think you should stop beating that pretty head of yours against a wall. The bird is just one of the many things that I don't understand about this place. But *you* understand, and that's what counts. So it's simple. The bird says he's your father. Then surely he won't play tricks with you."

"You forget," she broke in. "All Loko has to do is wring the bird's neck…"

Hank was thinking ahead of us both.

"He can't," Hank said. "The bird is a symbol known to everyone. But unless a symbol is visual it loses its significance. Your father was more than just smart. He gave himself the body of a bird the likes of which can't be found anywhere on this planet. Loko won't be able to find a substitute so he'll have to let him live. He will probably rig some sort of fol-de-rol about him being the only one able to understand the bird's words, or perhaps the only one who is allowed to converse with the bird. He can't afford letting harm come to the bird."

Of course my thoughts ran in an altogether different direction. I'd been puzzling over the bird without coming up with any satisfactory answers. Maybe I wasn't supposed to. But if the bird had been such a world-beater in the wisdom line, he hadn't proved it to me so far—and I wasn't sure I fully believed anything he'd said. Then there was that business of talking in various accents—all of which sounded like people of Earth. Of course with four or five different voices he would sound more mysterious I suppose. On the other hand, if he was so smart, how could he have left himself so vulnerable to capture by Loko? There was either something not very bright about the bird, or there was something too bright for me to understand.

Lovah whispered in an aside to me. "The Great Forest is at hand. Very soon it will welcome us."

I looked ahead and saw a wall of trees that stood so close together not a shred of light seeped into their depths.

"You could hide an army in there," I said.

"As I told you," Lovah agreed.

"But how do we get in?" I asked.

"The paavans will find the path. This is where we find them."

SHE spoke the truth about the panthers knowing their way. Straight as a line they sped for the solid wall ahead. As we came close, the place looked a little terrifying. We had to stretch out again in a single line. Luria took the lead, Lovah, with me grasping her close about the waist a little more tightly than usual, came next. I caught a glimpse of Jimno holding up his mount. I imagined he was going to cover the rear. Then we were in the damp darkness of the forest that was really primeval.

Strange cries rang out as we crossed the border between light and darkness. Rank odors filled our nostrils. It took several seconds for our eyes to accustom themselves to the gloom. Fitful rays of light seeped through the tangled foliage. But nowhere was to be seen a single area even a few feet across on which the blessed sun fell.

As we proceeded deeper I became aware of hidden creatures, some quite large, stalking us from the borders of brush, which were walls too thick to penetrate. Now and then one of these creatures let out a sound to betray its presence. There were roars that could come only from the throats of a paavan, shrieks that terrified because one didn't know or could imagine their owners. My hair stood on end for so long a time I thought it was starched.

"Where are we bound for?" I asked, and suddenly realized I'd spoken in a whisper.

"In a little while we will come to our trysting place," Lovah said.

She knew what she was talking about, all right. Quite suddenly the trees thinned and I caught a vista of an immense meadow. Then the trees closed in again. But as though the glimpse of the promised haven lent wings to the feet of the paavans, they sped forward with increased speed. Too much speed. Because when we passed the last line of trees we were traveling at such speed we couldn't stop or disperse. The ambush that had been laid for us was perfect.

THEY must have known of it. Or perhaps Jimno and Lovah hadn't done such a good job, or perhaps, more reasonably, they had tortured someone into telling the hidden secret. But they fell on us with the force of limitless numbers.

At least ten of them surrounded Lovah and myself. They were mounted on the monstrous lizard things. In the still-tangled brush before the open meadow, their mounts had the speed of ours. It was the pay-off, I thought, as I began to flay about me with the sword Lovah had given me.

The ones who surrounded Lovah and me were women. For the barest second I had some misgivings about using the sword in my fist. But only until one of them missed me with a wild swing. Then I swung. The blade went through her like a knife going through soft butter. Her mount kept moving forward and for a second her body hung together. Then the top half separated from the bottom and rolled off. But I hadn't time to gloat over it. These dames were crazy. They'd spur up and jab and swing, get in each other's way, all trying to knock us off at one time. Lovah's timing was excellent, though, and she wasted no motions in wild swinging. Every stroke of her sword was clipped and sharp. If only I wasn't behind her.

I proved the handicap. And the denoument. For in one of my wild swings I knocked her off balance. And myself off the paavan. I reached wildly with my free hand, tried to maintain a semblance of equilibrium, and in the end got neither and fell off. The women fell on me with savage screams of exultation. How I managed to fight my way clear of the forest of cleaver-like blades that thirsted for my blood is a mystery to me. But somehow I did, to get to a nearby tree. I wanted the protection of its thick trunk. I knew it was only a temporary respite. Still I could not give up hope.

That I did not escape to my temporary haven without damage went without saying. Why Hank and I had never exchanged our garments for the more protective, though scantier garb of the Polans, I do not know. But at that moment, with my back to the thick tree trunk, I wished we had. I was bleeding from several nicks and one gash; a sword had ripped across the flesh of my chest, splattering me with a crimson rain. It wasn't a mortal blow, only a flesh wound, but I knew that if I didn't receive attention it would prove damaging. Far more so than the other wounds I received.

My shirt hung by scattered slivers of blood-soaked threads to my body. One sleeve had been torn completely away. The blood had run down into my trousers, which were torn by the briars and looked more ragged than a hobo's. I sweated and stank like a draught horse on a hot summer's day. And I was besieged by a dozen women who thirsted for my life! The instant I was unmounted six others had come up on the run. I hacked away inexpertly, but with telling damage. And gradually the sheer strength I displayed won both their admiration and their respect.

I managed a quick glance around during a short breathing spell. We weren't doing so well. I could see any number of riderless paavans. Of Luria and Hank nothing… Then— they were at me again. Once more I took up the seemingly endless task. And this time it was harder. No longer did they come at me together, getting in each other's way, fouling up their sword play and making themselves easy marks for my blade.

This time they came at me singly and in quick succession. And on dancing feet. My swings were a little wilder, a little slower. I stopped after a moment and waited until one came in range before swinging. Again they changed their tactics. This time two came at me at once, one from right and the other from the left. And while I tried to keep both off, two more came from in front. I knew it was but a matter of a short while and they would wear me down. Nor was I wrong. Three times in a row I got the point of a sword in me, not deeply, but damagingly.

I HAD a last resort—my speed afoot. I *could* outrun them. Suddenly I leaped straight forward. I jabbed twice, missed one and got the second, and lost my sword in the maneuver. It went in too deeply and I had no time to pull it free. But I no longer cared. For coming toward me at a full gallop, was Lovah. I had lost sight of her after I had been knocked off her paavan. I could see as we rushed to meet each other that she too had not escaped unscathed from the fray. One arm hung limp, there was a bloody streak across the firm white flesh of her shoulder. But her eyes were ablaze and her face alight.

We were almost at meeting's point when I suddenly sprawled face downward in the marshy loam I was in. A creeper had tripped me. I struggled to get to my feet. But after two tries my knees gave way and I fell, rolling to my back.

The sky, seen through the filigree of black branches never looked so blue. Of course there were no clouds, just the cerulean blue that merged into the gold of the eternal sun. All this in the space of seconds. Then another something intruded into the scope of my vision. It was only a sidewise glance. Terror and death was coming my way. The most gigantic woman I'd ever seen was leaping toward me on huge splay feet, in her hand a sword fully ten feet long. Her expression was demoniac with transfigured fury. Her great breasts were bare and like those of monstrous cattle. I was powerless to move. The sweat was a sour river pouring down my face, saturating me in its stench. I felt a horror beyond words as she slid to a halt at my very side. Then the sword was lifted high above her head, her both hands clenched about the hilt. Eons went by, worlds were born and died, civilizations crumbled and death marched to muffled drum bets and stepped before me and bared its horrendous snout to my eyes and its cavernous mouth opened to swallow me...*and the sword shot downward!*

I heard the thin screech and swish of it, felt its cold breath on my cheek but saw it not. My eyes were closed for that infinitesimal instant. They opened and I saw its silvery length quivering and undulating beside my cheek like a frustrated pendulum. To one side stood the giantess, her hands tight about the blade of a sword that stuck out of both sides of her thick throat. She was trying to free her flesh of its grasp. Then her hands fell to her sides and a thick stream of blackish-blood poured from her mouth, her nose, her throat, and enveloped her in a redly-funereal garment.

"Quickly!" a voice came from above me.

I looked dazedly in its direction. There she was, my Lovah, a delight to my eyes and a balm to my soul and a saviour of my flesh. Her hand, firm and strong as a man's, reached down and took my lax fingers and hauled me erect. I let myself go limp across the thickly-muscled shoulders of her paavan. Her fingers, which fell lightly across my face, sent courage coursing through me. I bent my head back and she brought her face down and once more our lips met, not as they had before, in passion, but in the gentle caress of true love.

Her hand lay across my shoulder as we turned to face the enemy. Fear had been banished from our hearts though our arms were gone from us...

They surrounded us. They were many, and though they were armed and we were not, they moved carefully, as though they could not believe our state, or the fact that there were only two of us. We waited for their stings to bite us...

"Alive! Take them alive!" one of them called unexpectedly. "The man is the one who escaped the Pit!"

CHAPTER TWELVE

THE beast across which I lay stank to high heaven. I was bound hand and foot and lay belly down across its rump. Behind me rode one of the Amazons. Somewhere behind, Lovah rode prisoner also. Now and then we passed clumps of the dead, and though it was impossible to count them, I could see when the bobbing motion of the elk lizard allowed, that the greater part of the heaps of dead were Loko's people rather than Luria's. Not that I received any consolation from it. Now that I had passed safely through the period of shock following the battle, I could see again with at least a small measure of equanimity what lay ahead. The future wasn't very bright. For some reason I had stopped bleeding. I was on the weak side but at least I wasn't going to bleed to death. Hooray for me, I thought. They're probably saving me for a fate worse than death. I wouldn't have given a hang had it not been for Lovah.

Oddly enough our ride was shorter than any I had gone on willfully or otherwise. Whether my senses had dulled to time in this strange land, or whether the ride was truly short, it didn't take us long. The pueblos of Loko's town came into view shortly.

There were lines of people waiting our arrival. I could *feel* their hatred though I could not see them. I could feel as we passed through the oddly silent cordon of *hating* men, women and children, that we were the objects of their hate, and possibly of their revenge. I could understand it too. We, Jovah and I, were the symbols of the death many of Loko's people had met. Oh, it was true that *we* weren't directly responsible. But we were *here,* and we were prisoners. We rode a gamut there under the hot sun and not a finger was raised in our defense. I heard Lovah's first shriek of pain, her first outcry. There were no more: I suffered the tortures of the damned until we reached our goal. For from my own experience, I knew what Lovah must have gone through. They had used their fists, clubs, their teeth and nails and feet on me. Stones had pelted me until it seemed as though there wasn't a whole bone in my body. But I was damned if I'd let a single sound of pain escape me. And Lovah had allowed only the first cry to pass her lips.

Those were the physical things. There were dirtier, nastier things, ordure and worse that stung us. But at the end we came within the orbit of Loko's palace and some small measure of safety from the crowd. Our bonds were cut and even as I staggered around on stumbling feet I saw that Lovah was all right. But they gave us no rest. Once more I met the long halls and corridors of Loko's palace. And once more we were dragged before the dais on which stood the table and throne. This time Loko, Captain Mita and the giant warrior sat without their women. I gathered it was a change of time.

Loko no longer looked the benevolent old man. His face was no longer benign or wise. It was twisted in an expression of absolute rage. Saliva, white-frothed like foam had gathered at the corners of his mouth and hung suspended like soap bubbles.

"Little beasts! ...Animals! ...Traitors! She-devil and he-devil... You thought to make small of me...but my trap caught you. Ahh! That they did not make it strong enough for the arch-devil woman, Luria. But she will not escape long. Already they seek her... She will be found. By her hair, by her toenails will I have her dragged before me! And also her consort, the devil from another world! He didn't bring a magic more powerful than what I possess."

"Ah shut up!" I snarled up at the shrieking old loon. "You sound like you're losing your marbles. Not that you ever had any."

MY WORDS stopped the tirade. I thought I caught a gleam of admiration in Mita's eyes. But the old man had the floor and was going to keep it. Suddenly he grinned and I noticed for the first time that he had no teeth. I suppose if I was as old as him I wouldn't have any either.

"The fool teaches the wise," he said. "You are quite right, my friend…"

"Don't call me friend," I said sharply.

"I permitted my emotions the upper hand. But only for the moment. In anger. Now they must savor another pleasure. This one, however, I had promised myself on your first escape. I had thought to hold myself until I had your friend and the woman, Luria, altogether. But since that isn't possible at this moment, I will contain myself for the present. Of course I must have the satisfaction of a partial enjoyment. Slaves! The whips!"

I was too weak to fight. I was too weak to even stand. But I was damned if I'd give way. Not so long as there was breath in my body, or so I thought.

They bound us together face to face. Not just our hands and feet but strands of wire-rope about our waists and legs also. I could see the man who had the whip to be used on Lovah and she could see the one who was to do the dirty work on me. They shoved us around until they had us satisfactorily arranged to Loko's liking.

"Lean your head on my shoulder," I said. "If it gets bad, honey, take a good bite out of my shoulder, cry, sing, do anything but scream. I won't be able to take that…"

All the time I was talking I was waiting. I had an idea the old devil on the dais was going to give the signal for the torture to begin by a nod of his head. His mind operated that way. It was the reason why he had us placed in profile to those on the platform. He knew the psychological torture we were going through.

I had always wondered what could be the most terrible thing in the world. I found out then—waiting! Just plain waiting for anything. Especially when you know it's going to be unpleasant. I could get a very unsatisfactory glimpse of Loko and the others from a corner of one eye. It wasn't enough to define movements, or even to see the shake of a head, but I could see them. As the seconds dragged by I tried to turn my head to see more. The men who had bound us were masters of their art. So subtly had they wrought with the strands of wire rope that though I could move my head, it was only to the part of an inch. More, and I would strangle.

My attention was suddenly focused on the bronzed giant who was standing, whip in hand, behind Lovah. The muscles in his arms and shoulders were like those of some Atlas. He had stood impassive and immobile while others had pushed us about. Suddenly he flexed his arms, the muscles rippling, flesh-like-water. The immensely long whip coiled writhingly on the stone floor, as though it was a snake in agony. I saw then that the lash was divided in three parts, like a very long thonged leash. He raised the whip and moved it about. Faster and faster until it began to sing in the air. Suddenly he snapped it. The sound was like that of a pistol shot. Lovah, who was unaware of what was going on gave a startled movement of fear. I looked in her eyes and grinned.

"Gonna be tough," I said. "I love you, honey… It's a hell of a time to say that. But maybe it'll help."

"Love?" she whispered. "It is a strange word. But we have such a word here if I think it is what you mean. I love you too, man of another world. You are the first I have ever said that to. Nor will I ever say it to another. I was afraid only this moment. But now, why, it is as though fear never existed. Are we not together? Are we not bound to each other, body to body? Surely, if it is within the bounds of reason, so will our souls be bound. But not with strands of rope, but with the infinitely greater fibres of love, as you call it. Do not worry, man of mine, I will not cry out, though they beat me to eternity."

If I had had tears I would have shed them. If I had had the strength to tear myself from the prison they had bound me in I would have ripped their torture cell to bits and them with it. But I could not. I could do nothing but wait. *Wait... THE TERROR OF A WORD THAT BECOMES SOMETHING PHYSICAL...*

THEN there was no more waiting. The word had been translated into the deed. I heard the swish of the fibre snake. It made an eerie whistling sound as it zipped through the air. And hit...!

For an instant the shock was so great I could do nothing, say nothing. All I could do was *feel*. Once I had written of liquid fire being poured on someone. I suddenly knew how that hero of the pulps felt. Pain was like ecstasy, pain was like suddenly losing the world one was in and in an instant being brought into another world. I didn't even hear the sound of the second stroke. Only the feel of it.

Pain became translated into something else. Colors. First there was blackness. Just an oily pool of black into which your mind sank. That was with the first blow. The second brought a tinge of red into the blackness. After the third I stopped counting. Just the colors and the pain. Reds and purples and blacks.

The pain was something extraordinary. It always began with the area which had been hit, then spread. It was like the thin sound of a single violin string that's been plucked. The sound leaps from the thin wood paneling and spreads instantly in all direction. So with the pain I felt. Every single inch of me vibrated to the feel of the pain.

All of a sudden I heard a voice.

Well, maybe it wasn't a voice I heard. Maybe it could best be called a sound. Surely, I would have thought, had I been capable of thinking, nothing like that could be called a voice. It wasn't human, nor was it animal. I knew what it was, though. It was the sound of *pain!* It was the cry of the tortured and the damned. It was the sound of man being beaten, whipped, terrorized. It was the cry of all humanity wrapped up in a single throat.

Oh, do not think there is no limit to pain. There is. I began to develop an odd immunity to it. Not that it wasn't always present. Only it became pushed into the background. Taking its place, as though in compensation, a new world was conceived. It was a strange world. There were only three people in it, Loko, Lovah and myself.

The first glimpse I had of this strange world took place as though on a screen that had suddenly been shoved into my mind. We were in some sort of cave. The walls glowed redly from the reflections of hidden fires. Lovah, stark-naked, was dancing about a figure bound to a stake. She was brandishing a pitchfork. Another figure stalked in from off stage somewhere. I recognized myself. I watched myself move forward toward the nude figure cavorting about the stake and the man tied to it. Then I wasn't watching anymore; I was walking toward Lovah. She was singing a tune but the words did not make sense:

"Old Loko's hanging from a stake;
Old Loko's but a broken rake.

Soon he'll fry,
We must turn him.
Soon he'll fry,
Soon we'll burn him.
Old Loko's hanging from a stake;
Brittle bones, bones will break."

From ten feet off I took an immense leap, like that of a male ballet dancer, and landed beside Lovah.

"Ho-ho!" I chortled. "We have the old buzzard now, haven't we? My pet, I worked hard over the fires, but they'll make the labor worth it when we fry him. Have you pricked him to see how the juice runs?"

Lovah did a pirouette completely around the old man tied to the stake. She laughed gaily and a deep groan echoed the light sound. The groan came from Loko. At the sound, Lovah stopped dancing and I came close.

"Please," the old man said. "Spare this old graybeard…"

"Graybeard," I said in fine scorn. "Why there isn't a hair on that bald dome of yours and not even fuzz on your chiny-chin-chin."

"Rhetoric," the old man replied. "Merely rhetoric. A phrase. A passing thought. But, and this is more to the point, surely you would not harm an old, old man like me."

Lovah and I burst into delighted laughter. She whirled lightly about me and came to rest at my side, her eyes laughing up to mine and her lips inviting a kiss. I accepted the invitation. Loko groaned at sight of it.

"Oh, don't pay any attention to the old frastrate," Lovah said. "He's just jealous. He's just jealous because we're going to eat and he isn't…"

"Ho-ho," I laughed again. "He isn't going to eat. He's just going to be the eaten."

"Spare me! Spare me," the old man groaned.

"Spear him! Spear him, he says. *Spear himmmmm…*"

THE words died away in a long humming sound. The scene faded. The world of fantasy collapsed. Only the hum remained. I came back to reality to the sound of that hum. And found it was I who was making the sound.

"...Berk...oh, man of mine...please! Hear me..."

Her cheeks were dew-wet against mine from the tears she had she. Her voice was a sobbing entreaty that I could not deny. Strange, I thought, and it was the first time in the eons that had passed that I had been able to bring thought to my tortured mind. I could no longer feel the whip.

Her voice went on, her breath tickling my neck:

"...Stop doing that, Berk. Not any more. I can't stand it. I'll break too if you don't stop..."

"It's stopped, honey," I said. "Guess I went off the deep end. What happened? The guy get tired?"

Her head went back and her eyes were bright as stars and twice as beautiful. Her lips managed a smile. But two last tears coursed down the paths others had sown and hung poised, like wondrous jewels, on the curve of her cheeks. I would have given the breath of my life to lift my hands and brush them into a cup to hold precious forever.

"N-no. I think you fainted and Loko told him to stop."

"Well, that was nice of Loko. I can't say that I don't appreciate it. I'm puzzled, though..."

Her eyes asked a question.

"...My back," I said. "It should at least smart. But I don't feel a thing. Maybe I'm just numb from taking it?"

"No. They covered you with some sort of salve. I saw them place it on you."

"Ho, slaves," Loko suddenly announced. "Undo the bonds about the two but leave them bound."

They turned us so that we were facing the three on the dais. Then I saw another. The fourth was one of the women warriors. She was leaning over Loko's shoulder, talking earnestly to him in low tones, accenting with her hands actions she wanted to bring to light. The other two were listening absorbedly also. Loko kept nodding his head as though in agreement. After a moment of this she turned and leaped from the dais and strode from the room.

The three of them then brought their heads together and after several seconds of talk, Mita and the other also rose and departed. Loko then turned his full attention to us:

"I suppose I must forego the balance of this," he said. "Matters of state have come up. Of interest to you two also. The she-devil, Luria and the rest of them will soon be in my clutches. Perhaps it is best that I save the two of you for the time when there will be other rebels and traitors to keep you company. Throw them into adjoining cells so that they might hear each other's agony…"

THE instant the cell door clanged shut I rushed to the bars and called to Lovah:

"Are you all right?"

"Oh, yes. But now that the ordeal is at end for you, I feel this prison. We must break loose somehow."

She had a great idea, my Lovah. There was but one thing wrong with it. When Hank and I had been thrown into this clink they just left us there. Not this time. Directly outside our doors about midway between them stood a guard against the opposite wall. And now and then I saw the shadow of a marching man pass across the outside bars of our little cages.

"I think we're stuck here for a while," I said. "But always remember that 'what sticks you can get unstuck.' "

It was small consolation.

The sound of the warders who had brought us to our cells died away in the distance. The oddly quivering stillness of the prison settled on us. I started to turn from the bars to see what the land looked like on the outside when I saw our guard approaching. He placed his face close to the door bars and whispered:

"Loko is a traitor."

"Yeah," I said. "I know…" I stopped and the light burst on me. One of Loko's own men calling him a traitor. Hope kindled anew in my breast. Lovah must have seen the man step to my cell but she couldn't hear what was being said.

"Aye," the guard said. "A deep-dyed traitor. He has lied to us. The Holy Bird has said so. I heard it…"

"So?" I acted with reserve.

"It is not right. He tells the people the Holy Bird says he is the rightful ruler."

"So why don't you spill the beans. I mean speak up! Tell someone who can do something about it."

"He would have me killed," the guard said.

"Does anyone beside you know this?" I asked.

"Yes. My brother. He was with me when news of your capture came to him. He told the Holy Bird in his mean gloating voice about it. It was then we heard. Loko must have forgotten our presence."

"Where is your brother now?" I asked.

"He will relieve me soon," the man said.

"And you in turn will relieve him?" I asked.

"Yes."

"Do you think you can bring the bird to me?" I asked.

He shook his head that he could. I smiled but his face and eyes remained grim. "Loko has gone on the field. It is said that his forces have surrounded the rightful Queen, Luria. It will be some time before he returns. I will return soon."

Nor was it long before the brother showed up. He brought with him trays of food for us. The two of them divided up the time waiting on us, which amounted to their shoving the bowls into our cells and waiting until we were done. Then the first brother gathered up the empty bowls and went off.

I paced the cell in what seemed an endless procession until his return. He carried the bird in the open, and marched straight up to the cell, thrust the bird in on me and said:

"Loko will wonder greatly where the bird is. Nor will he know for a length of time. Perhaps by then he may find the means to escape him. Until then be at peace."

I WANTED to kiss the character. What a sweet guy. Be at peace. It was a long time since I'd heard that phrase. I looked down at the parrot on my wrist. The bird seemed asleep. Carrying carefully, I stepped out of sight of the man on the outside the cell. Our new-found friend had been careful to make the transfer during the time the outside guard was out of sight.

My bunk was below window level. I sat down and peered at the parrot. Suddenly one eye opened and blinked several times as though brushing the sleep from its lids. Then the other eye showed life also. We regarded each other without change of expression for several seconds. The bird was the first to break silence:

"You are perhaps the ugliest man I have ever seen," it said.

I hadn't known what to expect from it, certainly not that. I felt the heat rise all the way from my toes to my face. As if I wasn't having enough trouble, this scrawny thing had to give me more.

"Brother," I said. "Every time you open your yap, every time you make those kinds of cracks, you lose ten years from your life expectancy. Now why can't you behave?"

"The truth will out," the bird said.

"Nobody asked for it," I said, my voice rising a bit.

"I was just thinking of the future," the bird said. "The day of the woman is past. Loko can't lose. My daughter can but stave off defeat for a certain length of time. The inevitable must happen…"

A bitter laugh choked me up. For the first time since we'd come to this infernal place, despair bored a hole in my breast. This bird was telling the truth and we were going to pay the consequences. My hand fell and the bird hopped off my wrist and onto the bed. I saw then that its wings had been clipped. Loko thought of everything.

"…No," it went on. "Loko can't lose. Yet oddly, he can't win. A paradox, no?"

"Who cares?" I asked.

"You do," he said. "You want to live, don't you? The girl in the cell next door; she makes life worth the struggle, doesn't she?"

I lifted my head.

"You have been beaten, whipped, wounded. All in vain? You fought back, but you lost. Now you have a valid reason for fighting. I can see through the veil of time, but because the veil is not of one thickness alone, I cannot see all the way. This I can see. A level plain bound on two sides by a forest, on the third by a river and the fourth side by a deep valley.

"Two armies are drawn up on the plain. They clash and all is confusion, all is terror and all is lost to sight because they have lost their integral distinctions. They are mixed and are one. Now they separate into distinct groups, each fighting an individual war of its own. Now from the forest comes a new force. They are mounted on paavans and they are all men. They ride, like a spearhead of fate, into the thick of the warring groups. They ride close, slash off segments of these groups and ride off before retaliation can be given. At their head rides a bareheaded man with the face of an eagle. His eyes are alight with the look of a conqueror, and his set features have the look of judgment. Now others rally around his standards. He becomes a wedge driving his sword points deep into the heart of his enemy. They scatter and flee and from all sides are beset by their opponents and chopped to bits.

"Now I see something which was not plain before. A woman and man had been the leaders before. They are no longer there. They have disappeared. I see them again and they are bound to the mounts of a fleeing couple. The woman is unconscious…"

CHAPTER THIRTEEN

I DIVINED what he was trying to tell me. Luria and Hank... I rose and slammed my fist into the wall and the gray dust powdered and flaked around my fist.

"...They are met by a company of warriors riding toward the scene of battle. Now all turn and make full speed toward the rear. And in the lead is an old man, a man I once knew full well. Loko..."

I bent my head:

"I've got to get out of here!" I gritted harshly. "Do you understand? I've got to get out of here! And take Lovah with me."

"Once you learned your strength," the bird said. "Have you forgotten it?"

I lifted him to my shoulders. His clawed clutch bit deep into the flesh yet I didn't notice it. I waked straight to the door and clutched with both hands at the bars. Their coldness seemed to defy me. The guard looked at me with wonder in his eyes.

"The one outside will see you," he said with apprehension.

"Open the door," I said. "We're getting out of here."

I could read the indecision in his eyes. Now I heard the shouted warning of the one at the window. He had seen the bird on my shoulder. I couldn't risk waiting. Setting my feet firmly I yanked with a sudden pull in which all my strength was exerted. There was a ripping sound as the door was pulled from the stone and I staggered backward, the weight of the metal frame in my two hands. Hurling it to one side I leaped forward to face the astonished guard.

"With us…?" I asked.

He made up his mind. "Yes. My brother, too. Shall I get him?"

"Yes. Quickly! But leave me your sword and open the other cell first."

Lovah flew into my arms and buried her head on my shoulders. I let her rest there for a few seconds. I could hear the bellowing voice of the man outside grow faint as he sped to spread the alarm. But we had to wait the coming of the brothers. But they did not come alone. There were others with them, a dozen others, all armed and all willing to lay down their lives the instant they saw the bird. Lovah was given a sword, and with one of the brothers in the lead we started on the road to freedom.

"Where are we bound for?" I asked, as we ran full speed down the twisting lengths of the corridors.

"The throne room," one of the brothers replied. "Loko has returned with Luria and the stranger who came with you from the other world."

The news lent wings to our already flying feet. Then I noticed that we weren't running by the same path I'd been taken. Suspicion raised its head in my breast. As though reading my mind the one in the lead gasped:

"The other way we'd meet those coming to bar our path. This way is longer but safer."

He was right.

We rushed into the throne room from a side entrance, but one that was all the way at the far end. So intent were those in the room on what was taking place before the dais, they didn't even see us. I could understand their intent.

Hank and Luria were in the same position as Lovah and I had been only a short time before. The only difference being that they were not bound together. Further, they had been made to kneel before Loko and the other two. Loko was on his feet, a look of mad fury on his wrinkled face. His arms were raised above his head and I could hear the thin screech of his voice all the way across the room:

"You will not die quickly, I promise that. I will make life drain from your bodies as the sweat labors from it on hot days. I will have my revenge—I will make it last to your bitter end. They will come too late, and seeing your lifeless bodies will give up the struggle..."

HE STOPPED, warned by the shouts of the guards and the two men beside him. He took one look at us, turned and scampered backward to seek refuge behind his warrior men.

In an instant a solid wall of guards had been formed before the two captives. We hit them and it was like plowing into an immensely thick rubber band. We hit and bounced back. This time I took the lead when we charged forward again. I swung my sword like a man swings a reaper and whatever it touched became two. My men seemed charged with the same fury as I. They hacked and stabbed with terrible effect. But once more we were too few. Reason and sanity left me. I was a wild animal. Strange sounds came from my throat. Screams of madness, shouts of delirium. Fear was plain on the faces of those facing me. For a few moments they gave before my attack, enough for me to win to the sides of the kneeling man and woman. It took just the time of two sword swipes and they were free. Then they were at my side and swinging with me.

More and more guards kept joining in the fray. We were outnumbered fifty to one. But not for long. Suddenly there were shouting voices, voices that sent echoes of "Luria" echoing about the stone walls, and from all sides warriors streamed in to join the battle, Luria's warriors.

Our opponents melted from our sight, streaming to join their leaders in flight. But not for long. We had Captain Mita and the giant who had sworn to do things to Hank and me, to reckon with. Even from my small experience in this pest-hole I knew what a maze it was. We discovered it was a perfect place for defense. Each corridor had been built with that purpose in mind. Ten men could hold back a hundred in their narrow reaches. And there were dozens of corridors.

We had won the throne room. But we soon discovered that we had not won a complete victory. Loko was a long way from giving up the struggle.

Ever since we had been rescued from the tented compound where we had been prisoners, I had wondered why the use of bow and arrow had not been more universal. Later I was told that they had not as yet become proficient in its use. Loko's men were. Or those he had trained. Suddenly a hail of arrows met our advancing forces. It was only fortunate that we were not in the open. As it was, those barbed shafts kept us at bay. And once more it was Jimno who devised an impromptu escape from them.

"Small groups," he shouted, taking the play away from Luria as naturally as though it had been God-given. "Six and eight to each. Go low—and keep moving. Stab and go on. Don't let yourselves be targets."

As though they had been trained in the new maneuver for a lifetime, they followed the command to perfection. Now when a man or woman fell it was a single one and not as before, by fives and sixes.

But still it was hack and chop. Loko, or rather Mita, had enough sword fodder to keep us busy. I had learned a lot about the use of a sword. I no longer swung it in wild circles, hoping to catch someone in its path. Now I jabbed and chopped. My sword and I were covered with blood. Lovah, too, was finding revenge for the indignities she'd suffered.

At last the corridor we had found ourselves in came to an end. We were on the parapet that encircled Loko's pueblo palace. Our enemies were fleeing from us. For the first time I saw a means of escape that I hadn't seen before. Ladders had been placed against the walls. Men streamed like firemen down these ladders.

THE chase continued. But it was a little more even now. Now we were in the open where the archers had a chance at us. But they were not too proficient in the use of the bow. The arrows were indiscriminate in their choice of victims. And they found their friends as quickly as their enemies.

We won through the hail of steel and forced our way to the ladders. Soon, each ladder had its quota of Luria's warriors in command. Nor did it take long before we were on the stretch of ground below and continuing the chase. It was only then that we learned Jimno's genius.

He had thought of everything. From above came a shrill imperious whistling. And from the great grassy plain surrounding Loko's city came a horde of paavans.

I don't know how many there were or how Jimno had gone about calling them but come they did in an irresistible wave, which swept away all who opposed them until they arrived within the precincts of the city itself. Here they were met by those trying to flee. Pandemonium followed.

But all this is what happened at the shrill calling of the paavans. As for us, we followed so close on the heels of our enemies that they had little chance of cutting the ladders from us. There were a few who managed it, but not many. Those who were on the ladders at the time, friend and foe alike, met a quick death below, for the drop was all of seventy feet.

We won our way to the bottom. At our head Jimno strode like an avenging angel. I suppose the memory of what happened to his wife and children was never to be forgotten; nor would the enemy ever forget the flashing sword that took a dozen lives for everyone exacted of his. We followed close behind and chopped away after him. It seemed we were invincible. They fell as the leaves fall in the wake of a storm. They retreated until we backed them up against a rear wall of the palace pueblo itself.

There were a hundred of them against perhaps fifty of us. The odds were even.

We paused, all together, as though drawing the last breath and strength for the ensuing struggle; for it was in each of our minds that it was to be to the death. Then both sides leaped at each other. Whether by chance or intent, Hank and I were opposed by the giant and Captain Mita. Mita was my opponent.

All it took was a single stroke on my part to know that I was no match for the Captain's skills with his sword.. He parried my clumsy jab and had it not been for a stroke of sheer luck, the engagement would have ended quickly. His foot slid forward at the same time his sword did. But someone alongside kicked him while trying to get out of the way of a blow, and that allowed his parry to slide past me, just under my shoulder.

I leaped backward to safety.

I knew then I had but a single chance. Slash and keep slashing with the utmost disregard for safety and depend on his being on the defensive all the time. Sooner or later by sheer strength I might wear him down. It sounded good in my brain. It even started off well.

I whirled my sword so fast it was but a streak of light. And, as I had hoped, he kept on the retreat. But why was he grinning? Suddenly he stepped in—slid in would be a better way of describing the movement he made. He jabbed easily, somehow avoiding my clumsy blows. The sword tip pricked me and blood began to flow. Again and again he managed to evade my thrusts and slashes and every time he came in he departed with a little more of my blood leaking from various parts of my anatomy. He was toying with me.

After a while I began to gasp a bit. Breath was becoming harder to catch. He motioned me forward, saying:

"Come! You have only felt the tip thus far. The edge is keener, will make life depart the quicker. You have lived long enough. Soon your time will end…"

TO HELL with it, I thought. A guy can live but once. And Lovah or not, if my time was now, that's the way it would have to be. I dove forward again and by sheer force broke through his guard, making him retreat. I even managed to get in a couple of digs of my own, yet he always managed to evade the death thrust.

Once more I had to stop to regain a spent breath. I then realized what he had forced me into doing. He had retreated all right. But in the direction he wanted. And in so doing he had forced me to go along. Now his back was against the wall of the palace and I was in the sun. His sword danced merrily in front of my eyes and seemed to shoot sparks into them.

"You have courage, my friend," he said. "It is a pity that I have to kill you. But first I must kill that thing on your shoulder…"

The bird, I thought suddenly. It was still perched on my shoulder. Its claws still dug into my flesh and for the first time I felt the bite of them. Softly to my ears came the last words of the bird, Luria's father:

"This time death will be final for me. Tell Luria this world is done for her. And say that the world she will go to has no need of women warriors…"

They were the last utterance he made. In a movement that was but a play of light, too quick for my eyes to follow, Mita brought his sword forward with a gentle but lightning-like movement of his wrist. I did my best to leap out of its way. But the blade was not seeking me. It found its mark all right. A spatter of warm liquid struck against my cheeks and from the corner of my eye I saw the head of the Holy Groana Bird fall to the ground. Then I no longer felt its claws in my shoulder's flesh. The mystery of it would never be solved now.

"So be it," Mita said. "The time has come my friend. Now!"

He danced forward and his blade flickered toward me, now toward my throat and now toward my chest but always to return as I danced awkwardly aside. But he was no longer smiling at my movements. Suddenly he snaked forward, bent a little lower than usual and shot out one leg and arm in a simultaneous gesture. I made the mistake of following the direction of his leg. I don't know about this business of a drowning man seeing his life flash before him as he goes down. But *this* I knew…Mita's blade was about to take my life.

But suddenly there was a shadow—a quick moving shadow, followed by a voice calling to me, the voice of my beloved. But I had not the breath to answer—a pointed bit of steel was leaping to find a spot in my flesh…

My sword fell to the earth. My eyes were suddenly too tired to stay open, yet too horrified, too amazed to close. But I knew who had cast the shadow—Mokar. As though he had been shot from the blue, he had come in a tremendous leap to land full on Mita. One snap of those terrible jaws and Mita's life had escaped in a cascade of gore. Mita had spoken the truth. The time had come. *His time.*

I turned wearily. Just in time to see the last of the great drama. Loko was pinned against the wall not far from me. Hank was just stepping away from the headless body of the giant, Luria and Jimno were facing Loko, and Lovah was running toward me with the grace and speed of a gazelle.

I took her in my arms and she was limp for a second. Her fingers explored my wounds and her eyes lit up and her lips gave a sigh as she saw that I was only nicked.

We moved, arm in arm, toward the frozen tableaux.

Loko was pleading for his life, a broken stream of words that sounded oddly profane from lips that had caused so many to die. They were the sounds of a babbling idiot.

Luria was a pale-faced ghost, now that the die was cast. She saw that the bird was missing from my shoulder and at the nodding of my head knew it was dead. Her lips thinned and determination made her jaws go square.

"Throw him a sword," she said.

The blade lay at the old man's feet. He didn't even look at it. Begging words dripped from his mouth, broken-voiced promises that had no meaning. Suddenly Jimno pushed the girl gently aside, saying:

"It is not meant for a queenly blade to be defiled. His flesh would rot the steel, tarnish its color. He is but carrion even in life. No better dead, surely…"

Loko died more quickly than did most to whom he had ordered death…

" LURIA," Hank was saying. "There is nothing here for you anymore. Jimno has proven a right to rule. It's better that way…"

We were sitting about, the four of us, Lovah, Hank, the beautiful girl who had been the Queen, and I. Jimno was rounding up the last of Loko's forces. Lovah found the hollow of my arms and was content there.

"But my people," she protested.

"They will live and well, too," Hank said. "Jimno is wise and great. He is a poet, remember. But also a warrior. He proved that. He won his right to a kingship. Let the days of a woman's rule end."

She turned her face to his and he smiled and went on:

"Except for the rule over me. You have always been *my* Queen. In my heart you will always reign. But in my land, how much greater and more enduring will it be."

"I have the power," she said aloud. "Perhaps…"

We became tense as she turned and gave us each a look of intense search. Then her lips framed a smile and she continued, "Close your eyes, all of you. And let us pray we return to that place from whence you came…"

It was evening. We were in a large city. Skyscrapers were framed against the cloud-studded sky. We were not far from water. I could hear it slapping against a pier… Then I saw the white wonder of the *Wrigley Building*. We were home again.

* * *

LOVAH knows what it means to be a writer's widow. A week has gone by since our return. She has wanted to go out every night. But every night I say:

"Can't honey. Got to finish this for Ray Palmer."

And always the same words from her:

"I am beginning to think you married the wrong person. This Ray Palmer, whoever he is, is more a wife to you than I am."

I grinned. Only in one way, I thought. He'd never be in any of the other ways you are. Her arms slid around my neck. She whispered something to me, and Ray, manuscript, work, were all forgotten. Nobody cooks hamburgers like my wife…

THE END

www.ingramcontent.com/pod-product-compliance
Lightning Source LLC
Chambersburg PA
CBHW030309180626
46810CB00003B/984